Amabel Couldn't Understand Why Sean Should Be So... Jaunty This Morning.

The first time she'd ever considered a tumble, and he'd ignored all the obvious signs of her willingness. Was she so inept? Or maybe he just teased and enjoyed frustrating women? She'd thought men were easy.

Obviously, he was old enough and so was she, so what was his problem?

He was the Rocker. He was the one women clawed at and fought over. She ought to have known better than to offer herself. He was probably worn-out. Depleted. Incapable.

She shot a glance at him and intercepted a very amused look. He didn't look depleted....

Dear Reader,

For many years you have known and loved Silhouette author Robin Elliott. But did you know she is also popular romance writer Joan Elliott Pickart? Now she has chosen to write her Silhouette books using the Joan Elliott Pickart name, which is also her real name!

You'll be reading the same delightful stories you've grown to love from "Robin Elliott," only now, keep an eye out for Joan Elliott Pickart. Joan's first book using her real name is this month's *Man of the Month*. It's called *Angels and Elves,* and it's the first in her BABY BET series. What exactly is a "baby bet"? Well, you'll have to read to find out, but I assure you—it's a lot of fun!

November also marks the return to Silhouette Books of popular writer Kristin James, with her first Silhouette Desire title, *Once in a Blue Moon*. I'm thrilled that Kristin has chosen to be part of the Desire family, and I know her many fans can't wait to read this sexy love story.

Some other favorites are also in store for you this month: Jennifer Greene, Jackie Merritt and Lass Small. And a new writer is always a treat—new writers are the voices of tomorrow, after all! This month, Pamela Ingrahm makes her writing debut...and I hope we'll see many more books from this talented new author.

Until next month, happy reading!

Lucia Macro
Senior Editor

Please address questions and book requests to:
Silhouette Reader Service
U.S.: 3010 Walden Ave., P.O. Box 1325, Buffalo, NY 14269
Canadian: P.O. Box 609, Fort Erie, Ont. L2A 5X3

Lass Small

WHATEVER COMES

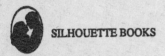 SILHOUETTE BOOKS

ISBN 0-373-05963-9

WHATEVER COMES

Books by Lass Small

LASS SMALL

finds living on this planet at this time a fascinating experience. People are amazing. She thinks that to be a teller of tales of people, places and things is absolutely marvelous.

To Cari and Rob, our daughter and son-in-law,
who live in Indianapolis

One

Amabel Clayton was distractively feminine looking. She was fragile, with a slender body that was marvelously curved. Her hair was thick and black. So were her eyelashes. Her eyes were blue. She ignored the whole image but, careless as she was, there was nothing she could do about the facade. As a reporter, she would have chosen to look less in need of male assistance, although there had been occasions when her look of fragile helplessness . . . had helped.

Most of her associates called her Clayton, but there were those who called her Mab. With a bird-dog relentlessness, she was one who immersed herself completely in her work, with no need for a social life. Since she forgot about men, she had been accused of not liking them. That wasn't true. How could anyone like or dislike something to which she paid no attention?

Living in L.A., Amabel was a West Coast reporter for *Adam's Roots,* the weekly newsmagazine crowding into the *Time* and *Newsweek* slot. It had been publisher Simon Quint's imagination that selected the name. As the roots planted in the past—by Adam—had to be dealt with, so it was that the roots planted today must be dealt with in the future.

When told of Amabel's new job, her father had frowned at her and asked, "You're going to work for Simon? He's as parsimonious as his name. Does he know you were hired?"

"Yes, to both questions. He was one who interviewed me in New York. He liked the piece I did on Rufus Baird."

Her dad responded thoughtfully, "At least he recognizes good writing."

Her mother inquired, "What will you do? What sort of magazine portion will you have? I don't recall much of women in *Adam's Roots.*"

"Simon Quint is surprisingly liberal. I'll report roots?" Amabel shrugged and grinned.

So her dad teased, "I have some crabgrass roots and some dandelion roots you could blast."

How many times would she hear something like that? But Amabel had already heard all the root jokes and her reply was serious. "I'm taking the advice you gave me long ago—be fair.

"My interviews aren't going to hatchet anyone or make them appear ridiculous, but they'll show the readers what the person interviewed is like, how they feel about things, what interests them."

"You'll be brilliant." Her father was a prejudiced man.

However, her mother just suggested, "Interview Sean Morant."

"An interview with him is impossible!" Amabel exclaimed. "The Rock Star of all time? And you think little old Amabel Clayton could snatch The Interview of the Decade? Pish and tosh."

But among friends her own age, that was the overwhelming reaction of all the women to her new job. How many times had she heard variations of: *You might interview Sean Morant!*

Her replies were fairly uniform about her chances being very similar to a sin-doomed snowball's. She got very tired of hearing about Sean Morant.

In the several years that followed Mab's hiring, she did well. Her research was meticulous. She was businesslike and tactful. Of those she interviewed, she asked reasonable questions and searching ones. But she asked no hostile questions or embarrassing ones. It wasn't her job to dissect a victim. She was completely fair with any age or any sex. She had very little trouble getting interviews. But she did not interview Sean Morant.

Sean's PR man was naturally charming. He was probably somewhere in his forties, some years older than Amabel, and he cultivated a low profile. He looked rather pleasantly anonymous. He'd chosen to be called Jamie. Jamie Milrose.

He told Amabel, "Of all the reporters in this world, my love, if Sean gave out an interview, it would be to you—you know that. But if he allowed you that privilege, then he would have to give the same courtesy to all the other clamoring reporters in this world, avidly after an interview with Sean Morant."

Jamie was patient. He explained, "You must know how many publications there are which would want that chance at Sean Morant! From *Adam's Roots* through all the variety of news to Fort Wayne's South Side High School. I went there to school, and I was on the staff of the *South Side Times!* So I know what it's like to be a reporter." With his expansive manner, Jamie gave her a lofty look, which invited her to laugh. She didn't laugh.

Jamie continued, "However, if that happened, if we should grant interviews so recklessly, think of it just in Sean's time spent! It fairly boggles the mind, doesn't it? And the wear on his poor vocal cords! Ah, my love, have pity. Give it up."

Enunciating with some careful exaggeration, Mab told Jamie, "I'm not your love."

"It's an expression," he soothed. "It's like a greeting kiss. It means nothing." He smiled slightly with his head cocked just a bit. "Are you really a man hater?" He was silent as he watched her.

With the same kind of patience Jamie gave to interview requests, Amabel replied, "I love every one of God's creatures. It's just that I love some more than others."

"Are you a lesbian?" He asked that deliberately.

"No." She gave him an enduring stare.

"Then if you aren't of that persuasion, how about dinner?" He opened out his arms in an expansive gesture. "I could change your whole outlook on life." He used his most practiced male grin.

"The incredible conceit of men is something to contemplate." She gathered up her things, put her pad and pencil into her purse and tried to close the zipper, but it stuck.

"We could discuss the interview," he invited temptingly. "You could see how much I know about the way to access Sean."

She paused in her struggle with the zipper. "I thought you said there was absolutely no chance."

"There isn't." He smiled. "But you could...try...with me."

"Jamie, you're one of the reasons I have no use for men. You never give it up."

"Now, now." He settled in to enjoy their word exchange. "What have I ever done to you?"

"Since I am careful, you've done nothing." She looked as if she was being very tolerant, but it was a trial.

He grinned. "You are a challenge."

"Forget it." She went back to the zipper.

"Why don't you interview me about Sean?" He took the purse from her, opened the zipper, stuffed a head scarf deeper and zipped it closed.

She hesitated. "How well do you actually know him?"

"You could find out." He handed her the purse as if it was a rose and his smile was wicked. "I have a nice little place up at Big Sur, just below Monterey. We could go there and lock...heads for a couple of days and see how things go." He gave her his honest look.

"There's a limit to the things I'll do for my job. I would welcome the opportunity to quiz you, but a weekend is out of the question."

He laughed, his eyes twinkling. "There was always the chance you'd be an eager young reporter prepared to give her all for the cause. Frankly, my dear, I hardly know the man."

Mab was taken with the thought that it sounded very like Clark Gable's classic reply to Scarlett's plea.

Mab had never done the "other people" format for an interview. It wasn't uncommon to seek out the opinions of acquaintances of well-known people. Or she could raid the files stored in the newspaper morgue for involvements and speculations about anyone in the news. It seemed the lazy cop-out to only interview the friends or relatives or co-workers of a personality...such as Sean Morant.

But Jamie had planted a seed, a root. And it grew and would have to be dealt with, for it would change Amabel Clayton's life.

From her meeting with Jamie Milrose, Mab did glean one little item that set off a furor. Among the personality briefs, in *Adam's Roots,* she reported there was some question about Sean Morant's vocal cords being in jeopardy. Would he lose his voice? If he did, what would happen to his group? What would become of Sean Morant?

With her succinct words, panic erupted among the Rock devotees. The item was picked up and spread. It was mentioned in turn on MTV, Music Television, who hoped the rumor wasn't true.

After a week had passed, Jamie called Mab. "You darling! His records are being snatched up—everyone thinks his vocal cords are doomed. Beautiful! I owe you."

So, quite naturally, Mab leaped on that. She quickly asked, "How about an interview?"

His voice a purr, Jamie reminded her, "There's always Big Sur."

"Jamie, you just said you owe me. What about an interview with Sean?"

"Would you like an autographed copy of his *Timeless* album?" Jamie inquired in a generous manner. Then he added smoothly, "There's a woman in 'She Rocked Me' that could well be you."

But Mab ignored the chatter and stuck to reality. "Jamie, you said you owed me. Try for the interview."

"'Tis hopeless, my love." Jamie was regretful, but that finished the conversation.

Several days later, Amabel got the autographed *Timeless* album, and played "She Rocked Me." She had never listened all the way through any of Sean's recordings. His roughened voice was what a woman wanted...she'd heard. The woman Jamie said could well be Mab used the man like a vampire, sucking him dry of innocence and love before she discarded him. It made Mab mad.

So the album was still on Mab's desk when her boss, Wallace Michaels, walked into her cubbyhole. He picked up the album and asked, with some startled interest, "You get autographed albums from Sean Morant?"

Automatically correcting his leap to an erroneous conclusion, she replied, "From his publicity agent, Jamie Milrose." Mab went on typing. She was allergic to computers.

Wallace asked her, "You got an in with Jamie?"

"Wally," she explained to an innocent, "Jamie probably signs the albums himself. He's that tricky."

He asked quickly, "Could you get an interview?"

Wallace Michaels was VP over all the people news of *Adam's Roots*. Since his job dealt only in personalities, he felt like a third-class citizen and was sensitive about it. He wanted to be in the mainstream of news and happenings and actually he was only involved in . . . gossip. He adjusted to the only way to handle gossip. He took it seriously.

"Wally, you know I have been trying to get an interview with Sean Morant for you for three years. I speak with Jamie Milrose several times a year in that effort. I have tried to waylay Sean Morant, and so far I've been unsuccessful. So has every other reporter. We get only the publicity handouts. You are aware of all that."

Wally pushed up his lower lip thoughtfully and declared, "We need an interview."

"Good luck."

"Now, Mab— It was your little squib about his gold-plated vocal cords that caused all this hoorah. Now's your time. And nothing is going on right now! So, unless some other country blows up another, we could get a cover story out of it! Do it."

Mab was disgusted and told Wally seriously, "It would have to be with interviews of others who know him or who've worked with him."

Wally was firm. "Do it."

"It'll kill my reporter's soul." Closing up her desk, Mab lifted the pull-out typewriter shelf to release the holding, spring catch in order to swing it down into the desk. It stuck. She tried again.

As if an oracle, Wally observed, "You don't like Sean Morant."

She temporarily abandoned her desk's problem in order to stand up and look at Wally. She was kind. "I haven't met a whole lot of men I do like." She became gentle. "I find men are overrated." She gestured. "The ones I've met tend to be petty, self-serving, egotistically immature and quite ruthless." She scowled. "They've

fouled up the world. Both politically and chemically."
She became logical. "And with Sean Morant, we have
the ultimate in uselessness."

"You are the perfect foil to find out if there's a man
under all that hype. Do it."

She sighed impatiently and went back to fiddle with
her stubborn desk mechanism as she said, "You are one
of the few men I can tolerate. This isn't really an assignment for me. I'm not into MTV, or Rock concerts, or
that type of music and I believe it's a..." She was distracted by her examination of the desk mechanism and
she jounced it.

"He is involved with the Feed the World's hunger
programs."

"Who isn't?" She bit her lower lip and strong-armed
the stubborn, probably male, desk's unmovable typewriter tray.

"You know, Mab." Wally had turned soothsayer.
"You're a genuine man hater. I'm glad I'm safely married. If I wasn't, I might try for you and you'd shrivel me
up." He reached over and effortlessly swung the typewriter and its shelf down into the desk.

She considered him thoughtfully. "I could live next
door to you."

"Ah, a magnificent concession."

"But spare me Sean Morant."

But Wally directed, "Do the interview any way you
can make it." With that comment out of the way, he
added, "Chris would like you to come to dinner on Sat-
urday. She is having her cousin over, and she'd like to
expose him to you."

"Expose?" Mab turned back to Wally and raised her
eyebrows. "You make me sound like chicken pox."

He replied kindly, "You look so easy, and it's just a facade. Looking at you the first time, anyone would think you're all sweetness and light, and you're a shock. Men can be very misled. Chris thinks Joe needs the kind of set-down you'll give him."

"I'm a serious woman. I dislike being taken for a dolly." Then she enunciated her rejection distinctly, "My parents didn't raise me to educate the male population on the rights of women to be people."

"Chris would take it as a favor." Wally's eyes twinkled. "And I'd love watching it. Joe's a revolving one. Anyway you look at him, he's a bastard."

"It sounds like a thrilling evening. No, thanks."

"He would be a better man," Wally coaxed.

She rejected the whole idea. "I couldn't care less."

"Then how about Friday? There'll be just the family. Chris has missed you. And you know I love you, too."

Mab studied Wally seriously. "You really want this interview, don't you?"

"How astute!"

So it was that, like any hack, Mab began to go through the files; and the information, speculation and lies on Sean Morant did collect . . . along with the pictures. There were all sorts of pictures. Studio or candid. He looked bored. He looked like a man who didn't give one hoot in hell about anything. The only time he didn't look bored was in those pictures taken he performed.

Those made Amabel thoughtful. He was an interesting-looking man. He wasn't handsome. His face wasn't that unusual. He was above average in height, and he was well-built, but many men are. His hair was dark, and lashes shadowed his eyes. She had read that his eyes were brown. The pictures of him performing were in vital contrast to those pictures taken of him on the street.

She collected some of his videotapes. She played them at her small, canyon house. The house was perched on a gully. Alone, she played tapes of Sean Morant on her VCR, so that she could listen and watch this person perform.

On stage, Sean did have a presence. His movements were—well—a pleasure to watch. He was a well-made male animal. He exuded maleness as he performed. He used his maleness. Deliberately. With calculation. He was a leader to the male viewers, and a lover to the female ones. He was what everyone wanted. Except Mab, of course. Mab was immune.

She would look at him, performing on the VCR, then lift the candid street shots up to compare his pictures to the screen. Away from music, he looked as if he was 'on hold,' uninvolved, disinterested. The pictures taken of him then showed his disinterest even in being photographed. He didn't turn from the camera or give a big celebrity smile. He simply looked at the lens as one would a post.

The candid pictures fascinated Mab. And it was those which caught her attention. Those with women. A multitude of women. Each picture was remarkably the same. Each showed Sean to the left, full-length, dressed each time in the same type of casual clothes. His hair was carelessly tousled. His sober eyes were on the camera in disinterest. And on his left in each of those pictures was a different woman.

The women were dressed variously, some smiling, some as sober as he. All were tall, lovely and walking in step with Sean.

Mab began to pin the lookalike pictures up on her bulletin board. Her plan board. Row upon row of the almost-identical pictures: Sean walking with another woman.

In viewing the pinned rows, it seemed obvious to Mab that Sean wasn't indifferent, he was *exhausted!* All those women! They would take a toll. He was only in his middle thirties. He seemed older. It was probably his lifestyle, eroding him.

She geared her article to expose Sean Morant, the womanizer. All those women were known. A few had been fans or relatives. Those pictures had been discarded, and Amabel concentrated only on those known personalities who had been pictured walking with Sean Morant. She interviewed each one of them.

It annoyed Amabel Clayton to find she wasn't the unbiased reporter she'd always been. She wondered if she'd reached burnout at twenty-eight. Why should she feel a hostility to the women who walked with Sean? Why did she feel such a strange... distaste?

The only other time she'd felt such antagonism to another female was in sixth grade when her best friend was caught sending a note across the classroom to Amabel's boyfriend. He hadn't *known* he was her boyfriend but her best friend had. The feeling then was very similar to what Amabel felt now. It was almost as if she felt jealous of those women she was interviewing about Sean Morant.

Wanda Moore was one of Sean's side-by-side women whom Amabel interviewed. The interview was in Wanda's bedroom. Wanda was in bed wearing a thin bed jacket. The indication being that that was all she wore under the satin sheet.

In a marked contrast, Amabel was wearing a shirt with a light sweater vest, a matching skirt, hose and flat-heeled loafers. Her hair was under a neatly tied scarf.

Wanda giggled and confided, "My name's a, uh, play on words, you know?"

Feeling uncomfortably obtuse, Mab asked through thinned lips, "Really?" in a quite indifferent manner. She waited with poised mike.

"It's like I want—more." Wanda giggled and squirmed as she rubbed her knees together under the satin sheet.

"More—what?" Mab questioned; by that time she was being deliberately blank.

"You know. Sex." And she rolled her eyes at the grinning cameraman.

Mab looked out the bedroom window and considered applying to woman a one-person satellite filled with plants to resow the diminished world. It was painfully obvious Sean's attraction to Wanda was not mental.

One of the more irritating responses was when Mab asked, "Tell me about Sean Morant. What is your opinion of him?"

"*Oooh!*" Wanda went into spasms of giggles and eye rolling.

"Could you tell us what you mean?" Mab inquired with careful seriousness.

"He's just *delicious!*"

Stoically, Mab could not resist, "Did you ever discuss world affairs?"

Wanda lost the giggles as she inquired succinctly, "Are you kidding?"

So Mab asked kindly, "Would you mind our taking your picture? We may use it with the article."

"What do you think this whole exercise is all about, ice queen!"

When Mab returned to her office and confronted her boss, Wally said, "But, honey, it's very lonely out in space."

"Don't call me honey."

"Well, don't get mad at me if Sean's choice in female companionship isn't up to your standards. I'm not guilty! I married Chris before I ever even knew you, and you approve of her."

Mab commented, "I have this terrible feeling you'd react to *Wanda Moore* just like the cameramen."

"How?"

"Flushed and laughing and restless."

Wally asked with interest, "Are you jealous?"

"My God, Wally!"

"Well..."

On her soapbox, Mab responded, "When women are trying to be taken seriously? And Wanda acts that way? Instead of Hillary Rodham Clinton, men tend to think of the Wandas of the world when they mentally picture 'women.' It's excessively depressing."

"Are all the women who marched along with our hero like Wanda?" He went over to the bulletin board and viewed along the lines of similar pictures.

"A shuddering number of them. His IQ must range between forty and fifty."

"He's a fine musician."

Mab agreed. "There are many flawed people God compensated with a brilliance in some talent."

Wally gave up on the pictures on the board to look at Mab. "How many more do you have to see?"

"Three."

Then he asked, "Have you tried the computer yet?"

"Don't push."

"You're the last holdout." Wally reminded her. "It will change your life."

"If God had intended me to fly, he would have given me wings."

Wally chided, "That's the argument for planes—this is a computer."

"Don't irritate me."

"You've been that way lately, with no help from anybody." Wally was kind. "If I didn't know you for a basic man hater, I'd think you had an unrequited passion for Sean Morant."

"Good grief." She looked up at Wally with wide eyes of shock.

Wally observed, "You're paranoid when it comes to machines—and men."

"I'll grant the machine half."

"It's just that you don't understand either one."

Mab gestured. "Of course I understand men. They are simple, basic creatures."

"We're human." Wally admitted that.

"Very."

Wally inquired thoughtfully, "Did you ever get any help with this problem?"

"I don't *have* any problem! I am content to live alone, I don't need a man to take care of me, I can support myself. The only problem I have with men is they don't understand why I don't want to hop into bed with them."

He grinned. "Again, I'm glad I'm already safely married to Chris."

"Me, too. If you weren't you'd probably be depressingly like all the rest."

"Simon Quint, too?"

"No," she retorted. "I find our publisher a perfectly rational human being."

As Amabel compiled the Sean Morant interviews, she noticed there was one characteristic all the women had mentioned. Sean Morant was kind. Amabel put that into her report, which was very cleverly written. She was subtle. She implied he was a womanizer who kindly spread his attentions as widely as he could.

The rows of pictures from Amabel's bulletin board were used for the magazine cover. All those row on row, almost identical pictures of Sean Morant walking with different women—except for the last, bottom, right-hand corner. There the picture showed a similar shot of Sean, but next to him was a female shadow and on the feminine outline was written: Who's next?

With that cover, the article inside the magazine was superfluous. The cover said it all.

When the time came, Jamie had a preview copy and he called Mab. "Shame on you. Do you think our boy will be pleased?"

"He should have given me the interview."

Thoughtfully Jamie chided her, "This is a cheap shot, my love—you singled out one small segment of his life, and you exploited him. That's too bad." Jamie tsked, enjoying himself.

Mab didn't laugh. "He can give me the interview, and I will correct any mis...conceptions. I interviewed all those women, and it was a bloody bore, they were that alike, but I wrote exactly what they said. That is an honest report."

Jamie's voice was soft. "You are heartless, love, I feel very sad about you. Why don't you come with me to Big Sur? I believe I can still save you."

"Lay off."

"I have to get on before I can lay off."

"Jamie, you are a bore."

"Ah, but I'm not vicious."

Mab retorted, "That article was *not* vicious. It was only the facts."

Jamie agreed, "Chosen, and applied with great care and skill. You do know you will now have difficulty in getting interviews? Stars have felt safe with you. Now they will wonder."

"You are exaggerating and you know it. You enjoy needling people. No one has any cause to worry about an interview with me." Mab was very serious. "I'm sorry the truth is distasteful to Mr. Morant. He should choose his company more carefully."

"He will. He will."

In the wealth of news constantly being printed, the article and cover picture of Sean Morant was no big deal. It wasn't received with cries of delight or outrage beyond those intimately concerned. Among those, interested reactions to the article were varied. Her publisher, Simon Quint, called from New York and said in his parsimonious way, "I was surprised by the article. The cover was brilliant. You should have left it at that. But the man is deeper and wider and more complex than you made him appear."

Wally said it was one of her poorer jobs and she shouldn't put it in the portfolio.

Her mother wouldn't speak to her at all.

But her father eyed her solemnly and chided, "You really weren't very kind to that man. If I didn't know your professionalism, I'd find myself wondering if you're fighting a secret, jealous passion for the man."

"Passion!" All Mab could do was sputter over how *ridiculous* that was!

However, she did get a trite thank-you note from Wanda Moore on stationery printed with voluptuous bunnies.

Mab didn't get a thank-you call from Sean Morant. She really hadn't expected one.

Two

When Jamie Milrose walked into his agency office the next day, his secretary said, "There's someone waiting for you. He didn't give a name, but he called you Sarge, so I let him wait in your office."

"No kidding." Jamie paused to relish the moment. There were very few who were still in touch, after the U.S. sojourn in Nam, who knew of his change in name, job and total character revamp. Those few were all cherished friends. Who would it be?

All the survivors in his group were forty-some-odd. They had been able to put Nam behind them. They were now spread out, very involved in their lives, established. They saw each other seldom but with great pleasure. Jamie opened the door with anticipation... and he drew a complete blank.

Jamie stared at the man sitting at his desk. The man

looked up from the *Wall Street Journal* and greeted him, "Good morning, Milrose."

Jamie couldn't recall ever seeing him before in his life...then he walked closer and inquired, uncertainly, "Sean?" Jamie's business with Sean had been conducted by mail and occasional phone calls from someone of the group. Jamie had met Sean once.

The lazy, husky voice was casual. "I believe it has been mentioned that, off the stage, I'm to be called Tris Roald?" With automatic courtesy, Tris rose and moved away from Jamie's desk to stand with his back to the window.

Prickly, Jamie thought as he raised his brows. It said something for Jamie that he didn't need to immediately sit in the chair of authority at the desk; he stood also and smiled in his non-army sergeant personality as he explained, "Forgive me. You have to realize I hear 'Sean Morant' all day, half the night and worse on concert tours. Had you ever been in Nam, you'd understand about brainwashing."

"I was fifteen when that war ended."

Tris's control and power were there. Jamie could feel it. Tris was a man who ran his own life. "Fifteen was young," Jamie conceded. "Then you can't know how it could be to hear something endlessly and be swayed?"

With droll humor, Tris denied that. "I have a mother who was an army sergeant in the Korean War. She was a strong disciplinarian."

"Was she now." Jamie laughed. "I have to meet her. We can exchange stories."

"I believe you would have the edge. Her war was an accepted one."

"Ah, yes." Jamie's voice was soft and his liking for Sean began. "How did you know I was a sergeant?"

"I research my people quite thoroughly." As he did everything.

Jamie nodded once before he asked, "To what do I owe this unexpected pleasure?" And his eyes twinkled.

"Did you clear that article and cover layout in *Adam's Roots?*"

"No, of course not." Jamie's voice was conciliatory. He knew with Tris's words that the man was irritated.

The soft, husky voice suggested, "Tell me about Amabel Clayton."

"An interesting experience for any man, she—"

"What do you mean by that?"

Jamie shook his head once. "Not your first impression. She looks like a man's summer idyll, but she's a staunch women's righter. She's also a damned good reporter. No one calls her Amabel...she's called Clayton or Mab. On occasion it's Mad Mab. She has asked for interviews, along with every other conceivable publication that can possibly call itself legit, and of course, as per instructions, I've turned her down—every time—although I did give her the publicity handouts."

The roughened voice was grim. "She's taken revenge? Just because I wouldn't give her an interview?"

"I doubt the article was her idea. Wallace Michaels is her boss and he does push for what's current. And not being able to see you, she was free to handle it any way she wanted." Jamie added coaxingly, "We could tell her about those women."

"I don't owe anyone any explanation." The mild tone was deceiving. Tris meant just that. The glint of yellow fire was in his brown eyes even with his back to the light. "I don't like being labeled a womanizer."

"The article will offend a few people—your mother, you, some of your good friends—but the great major-

ity won't be affected." Jamie was practical about it.
"This is 'typical' Rock Star stuff. It won't harm you. It
might cause irritation, with an increase in panting
groupies, but that can be handled. No problem. This is
a one-day sensation. In a week, it'll fade away. I prom-
ise."

"I would like a close look at her. I would like to talk
with the kind of woman who could be so judgmental."

"An . . . interview?" Jamie was startled.

"No. Anonymously."

"Ah? Let's see." Jamie went to his desk and flipped
through his appointments. "In two days there's a recep-
tion for reporters and publicity personnel at the Beverly
Hilton on Wilshire. As a sop to all the frustrated reporters, we give them—us!" Jamie grinned with real
humor.

"Would anyone recognize me?"

"*I* don't even recognize you." Then Jamie cocked his
head in disbelief. "You mean you'd go there?"

"Can you get me a badge?"

"You'd boldly go where no Rock Star has gone before? It would be madness, man!"

"I could be visiting from Indiana to see how the big
boys handle things."

It was the beginning of their friendship. "Where
abouts in Indiana you from, boy? I don't remember Indiana being in your bio."

"I've an aunt up near Fort Wayne."

"We're practically *kin!*" Jamie laughed. "I'm from
the actual city of Fort Wayne!"

Tris finally smiled. "I know enough about the city to
pass casual inquisition."

"I've a friend on the *Journal Gazette* who'll cover for
you. You can be their West Coast representative for the

day. No problem." Jamie hesitated thoughtfully. "Are you sure? It's a rash thing to do."

Tris's instructions were firm. "You would ignore me completely."

"If anyone asked me, I would say, 'Sean? Here? You're crazy! Why would he come to the lion's den?'" Jamie appreciated the idea. "It would be illogical enough—no one would expect you to be there."

"I'll go. What do reporter types wear? Something somber? Something flashy?"

"A suit. Tie." Jamie frowned rather absently. "Be professional. You'll see all sorts of dress, but since you're from Indiana, allegedly, you would dress. Let me put my mind to this—there must be an easier way for you to see Amabel Clayton."

"It intrigues me to do it this way. And the sooner the better."

"There's enough madness in the idea to please me." Jamie grinned in anticipated malice. "May I mention— later—that you were there?"

"No."

"It tempts me." Jamie coaxed for permission.

Tris's refusal was said flatly: "Don't even consider it."

"It would be such a joy to see some faces as I told it. I could do it confidentially. I would limit it to two. Mab being one."

"I'd fire you."

Jamie gave a gusty sigh. "No humor. None at all...at all."

So two days later, when the reporter/publicist meeting was scheduled, Tris drove a rented car to the hotel. The pressure in his life too seldom allowed him to be alone—there was simply never enough time—so he took advantage of any opportunity that came his way to be free for a while.

He kept a house in the canyon country, north and west of downtown Los Angeles. With the badge for the meeting delivered to him, there had been a picture of Amabel Clayton. She was "an interesting experience for any man." Those were Jamie's words. How could anyone who looked as she did be the shrew she must be?

He arrived at the Beverly Hilton Hotel, which is located on Wilshire Boulevard, west of Los Angeles, in Beverly Hills, seven miles from the Pacific. Tris handed the car keys to an attendant to park it in one of the garages. Then Tris went into the lobby, as he pinned on his badge and followed the discreet signs to the International Ballroom where the meeting was held.

There were close to a couple of hundred people in the crowd. There were more men than women. There was the subdued roar of conversation and laughter for they were almost all acquainted. It was their business to know each other.

Even in that crowd, she wasn't hard to find. She looked like any man's summer idyll, as Jamie had promised. It was a while before Tris could quit staring. It was odd the number of men who stood out of her reach but who looked at her with a kind of vulnerability. Look but don't touch seemed a tested rule for her. So although some women spoke to Amabel, all of the men did at least greet her. She was natural and courteous in her responses. Why did Tris find that so strange?

With the cover story firmly in his mind as a shield against her, Tris worked his way through the throng to her as he considered approaches. It had been a good many years since he'd had to approach any woman. All he'd had to do was say okay.

He tried one of the classics deliberately. He wanted to hear her screech. Pretending to be joggled, and with perfect timing, he spilled his drink right into the open collar of her blue shirtwaist dress. He apologized, "I am sorry," as he handed her a clean handkerchief.

"Don't worry." She busied herself with the mop-up. "I buy my clothes with this sort of thing in mind. But being only February, it *is* a little early in the season for an unexpected dousing."

Her reaction puzzled him. She was lovely, courteous and kind. That wasn't his mental image of Amabel Clayton. He said, "Back home in Indiana," and he had to prevent himself from singing the line, "we don't drink cocktails this early in the day."

She held her dress out from her very nice chest and inquired, "What do you drink in the early afternoon?" And she raised those black fringed, blue eyes up to his and smiled just a little. Then she sobered and her eyes went out of focus as the most amazing shiver touched her core.

Without really paying any attention, he replied, "Lemonade under a sycamore tree."

"In February?" Her reporter's training saved her from the bemusement. "In Indiana? The spring thaw hasn't even started."

"February in southern California is a fooler. You forget how the top half of the country lives. In February all us Indiana farmers are down yonder, by the Rio Grande, sitting in the sun in trailer lots. They call us Winter Texans or Snow Birds, since we tend to migrate like birds to escape the northern winter."

"How did a farmer get in here?" She moved one hand to indicate the ballroom and that meeting.

"Yes. Well." He thought rapidly and replied, "I never actually farmed. I went to school and learned to read and write, and I'm a reporter in the metropolis of Fort Wayne, home of Mad Anthony Wayne, who licked the British."

Taking anyone called Mad Anthony's heroic deed literally, she expressed great astonishment. "He licked them? Why would he do a gross thing like that?"

Quite gravely he replied, "It wasn't with his tongue, it was in the War of the Revolution."

"And he was mad?"

"Probably because the British weren't being nice." He considered her damp dress. "He's the one who said, 'My country, right or wrong.'"

Fully realizing she was playing straight-woman for him, she asked, "Why did he say that?"

"More than likely his country was doing something he didn't entirely agree with."

"On occasion, I've had that very feeling."

"We are members of the same club."

It wasn't until then that she laughed. "Are you new on the Coast?"

"And new in the world of journalism," he agreed with complete honesty. Then he told her, "My name is Tristan Roald, but since that sounds like a contender for the throne, I'm called Tris. And on occasion that comes out Chris with a good many of the uninitiated." Since it really was his name, his eyelids didn't flicker, nor did his eyes shift even the least little bit, as he watched to see how deep her research had been, and if she'd discovered that fact about Sean Morant.

"Tristan Roald sounds like a Viking."

"We tend to take that very seriously." He nodded with the words quite emphatically. "Plunder and all that sort of thing."

"I'm Amabel Clayton and I'm—"

He interrupted in his lazy, husky voice. "You wrote the cover story on the Rocker. Uh, what's his name."

She supplied the name easily. "Sean Morant. If you don't recall that name, you must not be into Rock."

Adroitly he avoided a reply by saying, "The cover was impressive. Do you really think he managed so many women in that short a time?" He began laying his trap.

"Pictorial proof."

"You don't think it might have been just circumstances? That he's an actual innocent?"

She grinned.

To cover his face, he scratched his nose, since she was looking at him with thoughtful eyes, but he went on, "The pictures were taken," he conceded. "But he might not have even been very well acquainted with those women." He pretended the comment was casual. He had to hear her reply.

"I believe it's the exactness in the duplication of the pictures that got to me. He always looks the same, his clothes, his designer-tossed hair, his expression of boredom. Only the woman is different. It's time for another picture. The time lapse seems almost measured. It's as if Sean yawns and grumbles, 'It's time for me to be photographed with another bimbo.'"

He smoothed a hand over his hair to be sure it was all still neat and orderly, and he questioned with raised brows, "Bimbo?"

Amabel groaned. "I had to interview them. One does wonder why he chooses them." Then she had the grace to blush rather vividly and sputter, "Well, I mean, I suppose..." And she just coughed and tried to change the subject.

But he wouldn't allow it. "You think he just chooses a body for...physical reasons." It wasn't a question.

"It's not for conversation." Her reply was so positive on that score that it sounded a little heated.

"Do you have an unrequited desire for Sean's body?" His eyes were almost hidden by his lashes, but she could see the glints of golden laughter in them.

"I have the strangest feeling I know you."

"Ever been to Fort Wayne?" he inquired with honest candor.

"No. I am going to Indianapolis in March for a Women's Seminar—"

"I'll be just north of there, in Fort Wayne. Where is the seminar?"

"At the Hyatt."

"Ever been to Indiana? We've lots of wonders to see." And he had eased her past talking about who he might look like—or indeed, who he might be.

They talked of hotels, Indiana, California, people, and she introduced him to several people as Tris. Two asked if they knew him. Was he a publicist? He looked familiar somehow. He replied, "Well, if you've ever been to Indiana there are a good many of us around, and we tend to have the family look. My mother was a Fell, and her family were Davie and Hughs. And there are some..." But oddly enough by then the questioner had lost interest.

At the buffet, he crossed glances with Jamie and gave him a bland, vague look of a stranger. Jamie coughed then choked quite hard, and he had to be slapped on the back.

Tris said to Amabel, "He's probably drunk. Most reporters drink too much. Do you?"

"He isn't a reporter—in fact he's Sean Morant's publicist. No woman drinks too much if she's as opposed to men as I am."

"Now why would you be opposed to men?" he inquired in great surprise.

"Basically... Well, that word says it all. Men are very basic."

Tris snagged them each another drink from a passing tray—carried, of course, by a waiter—and he handed one to Amabel before he lifted his as he said, "Here's to the good old days, when men were men and women were barefoot and pregnant."

She refrained from sipping the drink and cautioned, "I can see we need to talk about women's rights. I do believe you've been somewhat out of touch? And that's especially bad for a news—"

But then a sly and droll woman's voice interrupted, "You still here, Mab? I thought you had left."

"Not yet." And Tris was delighted to see Mab blush faintly. "I'm still here."

And the woman eyed Tris as she replied in very slow, drawling tones, "So I see."

Amabel ignored that and didn't introduce Tris but asked him, "Has our sunshine staggered your physical balance and given you a cold? You're a little hoarse."

Tris replied quite easily, "All hog callers are hoarse." And with some pleasure in his own ready tongue, he added, "Pigs are deaf."

"You've said you were never a farmer, and since you're new to the newspaper business, what did you do before? I have such a strange feeling I know you. Have I seen you somewhere?"

"Interesting you say that. It's the oddest thing, but women often say that to me. Maybe it's our past lives, my Viking ancestors raiding villages and carrying off women, and there's now a basic, genetic fear of me." He smiled. "Are you afraid of me?"

And that strange shiver shimmered inside her from her core to her nipples. She glanced aside and decided it wasn't Tris; it was the damp cloth on her chest. She asked, "Have you been in porno flicks?"

"Do you watch them?"

"No, of course not." He puzzled her and she was a tad impatient as she went on. "But you seem reluctant to tell me what you did before you began work on a newspaper."

"The *Journal Gazette,*" he supplied the name as if to her inquiry.

She accepted that. "Before you began to work for the *Journal Gazette,* what did you do?"

"Is this an interview?" His eyes glinted. He was enjoying himself.

"No, of course not."

"I'm perfectly willing, you know. This is your great opportunity." He gave her a wicked smile. "If there are any questions at all, I'll answer them truthfully. Fire away."

"What did you do before you began reporting for the *Journal Gazette?*" She pretended to get out a pad and poised an invisible pencil as she looked up, elaborately attentive.

"I am only just associated with the *Journal.* I have yet to turn in my first article." All true.

"And . . . *what* did you do before that?"

"A multitude of things, nothing with any future. I've been the background for *Vogue* fashion models a cou-

ple of times." That was true. "I've helped do a Public
Broadcast conservation tape." That was true. "And I'm
a poet." He wrote lyrics.

"Make me a poem."

"Uh, there once was a woman named Mab, who with
men would flirt just a tad, but when it came to brass
tack, she would just turn her back, and leave the men
weeping and mad."

She laughed. "Limericks are easy."

"Poems take longer. Anything worthwhile takes
longer. Like friendship." He watched her. "Snap judg-
ments are generally a disaster. I'm a good man." That,
too, was true.

She sobered. "Did I give the impression I thought you
otherwise? I don't know you well enough to make such
a decision."

"Very true." His face was serious.

"And do you think I am really as heartless as your
limerick?"

He smiled. "I'll find out."

"We were speaking of women's rights," she began.
"After all this time, in our struggle, and with you being
in the newspaper business, it seems incredible you can be
so out of touch." She was amused by his rash stance.

He didn't bend. He replied, "You'll be glad it's over.
It was nonsense. Thank God you all have come to your
senses!"

"God is on our side," she countered.

"If you tell that old, old joke about God being a
woman, you're going to make me cranky."

They looked at each other, and although they smiled,
amused by their chatter, their bodies moved almost as if
they were squaring off for some kind of combat. He
understood it, but she wasn't really aware of more than

the feeling. Both felt the strong attraction between them
and each had a very good reason to be wary of the other.

She was cautious with men so that around her there
was a solid wall of protective reserve, but while she felt
he was a male threat, she saw the humor and attractive-
ness of this Tris Roald.

He had a very unfair advantage in knowing her iden-
tity when she didn't know who he was; but he had the
greater reason for his calculation. He intended to teach
her a lesson. He excused himself, saying he had to make
a phone call—and it was with a satisfaction, of hunter
for prey, when he saw she was still there waiting for him
when he returned.

They didn't see anyone else in that crowd, as they
sipped the wine and nibbled from the elaborate buffet.
Mab only spoke to others who spoke to her. No one
spoke to Tris, for no one knew him.

The two laughed and talked. She teased him, saying
she was one of three non-Indian "natives" living in Los
Angeles, everyone else was immigrant. Then she added
the truth, telling him in actual Los Angeles, her family
really went back only two hundred years. "My great-
grandfather jumped ship on the way back to Boston.
Ezekiel was a misfit, from the stern and rockbound coast
of Massachusetts, who apparently wasn't spoken about
as kin by that branch of the family until after World
War I!

"Ezekiel very boldly stole a Chinese girl from the
ship's hold. And he lived with the girl here in the sun of
southern California. They had *fourteen children*, all of
whom lived. He was a shrewd Yankee trader and he did
excessively well."

Tris nodded, watching her face. "Our families have
much in common. Adventure, independence and trade."

She agreed as she said, "And apparently a love for the written word. That grandfather had also stolen the captain's pocket Bible, and his two-volume set of the works of Shakespeare. A family story tells to what lengths Ezekiel went, in order to eventually trace down the captain, to return the carefully kept books. Charming. Very sentimental."

With his steady eyes on Amabel, Tris commented, "Another thing we have in common—honor. Our good names. Ezekiel had to clear his books of his theft. Did he also pay for the Chinese girl he stole? He did marry her?"

She thought Tris looked rather stern. He had a hard chin. She would hate to cross him. But there was that strange quivering deep inside her. And now even the surface of her skin seemed to feel him.

She blinked back into focus and replied readily enough. "According to the family Bible, they married soon after the seventh child was born. The family never mentioned the delay in Ezekiel's marriage. I discovered the fact one rainy day, in browsing through the names and dates, and called my mother's attention to it.

"She said preachers weren't always available for the niceties and, on occasion, emotions could get entirely out of hand—and *these* weren't *those* days and I should behave myself! To remember Ezekiel's stolen wife."

Amabel smiled a little before she continued, "I used to wonder about Ezekiel's wife. She probably didn't have any idea what in the world was going on when he snatched her and jumped ship. Then to be in a strange land, with a great bear of a bearded man whose voice rumbled sounds she couldn't comprehend. Did she want to be with him? He was obviously friendly... fourteen children! But what about her?"

With no hesitation, Tris explained it all. "In olden days most captive women were chosen by the men, and women adjust well to captivity." He slowly licked his lower lip as he glanced down her still-damp body.

"Spoken like a Viking." She shook her head chidingly. "Why are you brown-eyed and dark-haired? And not even six feet tall? You must lack a whole *portion* of an inch!" She smiled sassily.

"We ranged far and wide, and differences have always intrigued men." He reminded her, "Ezekiel chose a Chinese girl."

"You think he gave her much thought?"

"A man that bold wouldn't just take what was handy. It would be his choice. Any man who would—borrow—such reading material would be a sensitive, romantic, loving man."

"How nice of you to soothe my worry about My Ling."

"That was her name?"

"We aren't sure. He always called her that and spelled it M Y. Her name could very well have just been Ling. And it was the possessiveness of a thief which made him call her *his.*"

"I like Ezekiel."

"Men would. He forced his own life to be as he chose it. And dragged that little Chinese girl along. He was a formidable man from the stories handed down. But women shiver a little over being stolen. Women are very vulnerable. Men have directed our lives for all time. We are just getting to the place where we have a toehold in guiding our own fates."

He dismissed her words. "It's only natural for men to control women. My dad used to remember about the olden days when men had it all. I never thought things would get back to normal in my lifetime.''

She watched the wicked, golden glints of humor that betrayed him, and she smothered a smile in turn. "I'm going to run for an office in NOW."

"Now? This year? Here in L.A.?"

"In the National Organization for Women."

He gasped with some flair. "*National?* It's spread that far? That sounds serious!"

She shook her head and sighed, gustily patient. "I believe we need to talk."

He smiled. "Anytime. I'll be glad to instruct you on the woman's place in the overall scheme of world affairs. And yours in particular. I have a car, may I take you home?"

"Now what is the great-granddaughter of a captive Chinese girl supposed to reply to a descendant of a Viking under such circumstances?" She laughed as if it was cocktail chatter.

He replied easily, "Chance is a great determining factor in our lives. Each thing that happens nudges people into actions they wouldn't have taken. Like my being here. It's exactly the reason Simon Quint named his magazine *Adam's Roots*."

"You believe in fate?"

"You can call it fate, or kismet, or destiny or revenge."

"I can't believe you read horoscopes."

"My life is self-determined. I do as I choose. I follow the paths I want to follow. May I take you home? I must leave now."

"That's a rash offer in this area. I could live fifty miles cross town. But you're lucky—you don't have to back down from your offer. I live just west of here in the Canyons." She gave the address.

He said, "I'm staying at a house in that area. I believe you're just on my way. Let's go." His smile was rather strange, and it did give her some pause, but she shrugged it off and they left.

As they walked from the room, he removed his tie and put it in his suit pocket. Then, using both hands, he ruffled his hair before he unbuttoned his shirt several buttons. He took off his suit jacket, unbuttoned and folded up his shirtsleeves, and slung the jacket over his shoulder very casually.

The photographer was there just outside the entrance to the hotel, and the pair looked up blankly as the pictures were snapped.

Amabel asked Tris, "Why us?"

"They may know who you are."

"I'm not newsworthy," she scoffed.

"Your article created quite a stir. You're probably doomed to a life as a camera-dodging celebrity."

"Don't be silly," she replied easily.

"It happens to the best of us."

Three

With perfectly ordinary courtesy, Tris drove her home. Their conversation was pleasant. He drove well. Her body watched his. She had never been so intensely aware of a man as being male to her female.

Almost shyly she asked him in for coffee. He declined with a fairly standard semblance of regret. He saw her to her door, said goodbye and left her standing there, rather pensively, as he drove away.

She was disappointed. She went inside the little house, which perched recklessly overlooking the gully below, and she prowled through her few rooms wondering why she would be just a little irritated with Tris Roald for being smart enough not to prolong the day's visit.

He was wiser than she. Anything can be overdone. Much longer and they might find themselves wearing on one another.

But she really hadn't had enough of him, and she felt a puzzling lack or vacuum with him not there. She didn't encourage her brain to examine any reason for that feeling.

It would have been nice if they'd sat on her small terrace, looking out over the gully as they watched the sun setting on beyond the hills.

The problem was, he hadn't mentioned the possibility of seeing her again. What if he went back to Indiana and never gave her another thought? And she remembered the misguided photographer who had taken their picture. She wondered who it was. She would like to have had a copy of it.

It was Wally who brought the advance copy of *US* magazine into Amabel's office within the week. On the cover was the picture of Sean Morant and Amabel Clayton exiting what was obviously a hotel.

Their pose was the requisite one. He was on the left, casually dressed, his hair designer mussed, his face to the camera and his eyes blank. Next to him, on the right, was Amabel, her damp dress soft on her nice bosom, her face equally blank as she looked at the camera.

The tag line read, "Who's next? It's Amabel Clayton!"

At first glance, she thought it was a trick perpetrated by the staff there in L.A. on the order of a Harvard Lampoon. So it took a little while for her to realize it was an actual cover and one that was going to be on the stands for everyone to see.

While she remembered the cameraman outside the Hilton, she became vividly aware of the fact that Tris was Sean Morant. He'd deliberately set it up. She remembered the way he'd ruffled his hair, taken off his tie and shrugged out of his suit coat. And she remembered his talk about appearances being deceiving, and honor—and revenge.

Vengeance is Mine, sayeth the Lord. But this time Sean had helped.

He had his revenge. It was too bad he wasn't there to witness it. All the kinds of comments and smiles sent Amabel's way that weren't particularly nice.

Jealous women smiled and their eyes were sly. But the men! It was as if Sean's revenge gave each of them a little triumph over her.

He'd been so charming. So attentive…as he'd set her up for his revenge. She remembered her body's reaction to his and how aware even her skin had been of him. It hadn't been attraction; it had been a *warning!*

She endured. The magazine was distributed, and she had more copies of that picture than she'd ever dreamed when she'd wished for just one. They couldn't just have the glee of the sassy cover and a poke at *Adam's Roots.* No, there was a story.

Their interviews were with people on the street. Instead of replying to the interviewer's question, most asked, "Who's she?" And one said, "Not up to his usual standards."

That hurt. Jamie was quoted as saying, "They're just good friends." Of all people, he knew she didn't even know Sean Morant, whose real name was Tristan Roald.

So it was days before she even considered the courage it had required for Tris to walk into that maelstrom of publicists and reporters just to meet her and set up the photograph.

That had to have been the telephone call he'd made, and he'd timed it, saying he had to leave right then.

How could he have done that to her? What difference did the multipicture cover make to him? Why was he so angry with her that he would take such calculated revenge?

He'd actually been in all those pictures. She had interviewed all those tiresome women.

No one gave her any sympathy. More than one woman ignored the implied relationship, of the pair leaving a hotel, and expressed envy for her having met Sean—however and whatever.

Mab didn't blab his real name. Although sorely tempted, she considered that sort of backlash as beneath her professionally. But she felt noble about not doing it. And she hated him.

Tris didn't feel the satisfaction he'd expected and his conscience twinged. He'd wanted to teach her a lesson but he hadn't expected such a reaction for her, to her, about her. He suspected he'd been too rough. He could have... Well, it was done.

As with any exposure to public consideration, the incident quickly passed. In a few days it had faded. It was overlaid with all the other things about other people which went on in the rest of the world.

But it festered in Amabel. She spent a lot of time as she argued with a phantom Tris using reason and wide arm gestures.

"What's going on with you?" Wally asked one day.

She looked up at him. "Nothing."

Wally frowned at Mab. "You act unhappy. It's not still that cover, is it?"

"No, of course not."

"It's funny, if you look at it right."

Her responding, "Of course," was rather dull.

"You don't sound sincere."

She gave him a look.

"Are you going to Indy next week?"

"You know I am. What's the matter, are you running out of things to say?"

"Pretty much." He bit thoughtfully into his lower lip and watched his feet shift and then he told her, "There's a concert in Fort Wayne just about that time. I wonder if you've ever been to a Rock concert?"

She was cautious. "Rock concert?"

"Since you're not a devotee, it might make a very interesting viewpoint."

"Let me guess. It's Sean's?"

"Why, by George, it *is!*" His surprise wasn't well done.

"Cute. I won't do it."

Wally mentioned casually, "I got the ticket from Sean." He flipped it onto her desk.

She looked at the envelope as if it was a snake.

"It's sealed. The courier said there's a note inside. Read it."

She wouldn't touch it.

"Mab, you know I'm partial to you. Chris loves you and that by itself would be enough to influence me, but I admire your work and I believe you're one of my best—"

"What sort of horror are you working up to?"

Wally was chiding. "Now, Mab! Whatever gave—"

"*No!*"

He waved his arms. "How can you refuse when you don't even know what I'm going to...suggest?"

"I *know* what you're going to suggest! And I will not!"

"Now, Mab, you can do it. This little exchange between *US* and us could develop into a nice Hope/Crosby kind of humorous conflict. It would be good for circulation. All you have to do is go to Fort Wayne and see the concert. Then you tell us what it's like. See?"

"Sean's." Her look was deadly.

"Well, it just so happens you'll be in Indianapolis *any*way, and he'll be up in Fort Wayne. It's only a hundred miles. There are planes and airports out there in the wilds of Indiana and very excellent highways, if you'd want to drive."

"I won't do it."

"Mr. Quint thought it a good idea."

"He's out in New York."

"I know that." Wally scowled at her.

"You suggested this, didn't you."

"With the *US* magazine cover we could bounce back with the article and have a neat little thing going here." He smiled beguilingly.

"How can you ask it of me? I thought you were my friend."

Wally observed critically, "The tremble in your voice is touching. You do that well." But then he warned, "If you let a tear leak out, I will insist on a personal interview with Sean, if you have to pretend to be a bellhop!"

"Wally!"

"Even *Chris* is excited about this!"

"I'm going to apply for the space capsule."

"Fine. Right after you do the concert. Then we can work in something about unrequited passion on your part and milk this dandy little incident as far as we can go."

"I don't see how you can do this to me."

He shrugged and said the obvious, "Circulation."

"You are a nasty man." She glowered at him.

"Coming to dinner Friday?"

"I believe Chris should divorce you. I doubt she has ever suspected what you're really like."

He smiled. "You're a reporter. You'll do it because you know it'll make good copy. We got a glossy of the picture. We'll rerun a copy of the cover, then the *US* cover and then your story. Hot *dog,* this'll be one for the books."

She smiled in an icy manner. "I want a raise."

"Mab, don't get hostile on me."

"Do you realize the reason I'm going to Indianapolis is to speak at a Women's Seminar? Then I'm to go to Fort Wayne and witness a Rock concert! Tell me this can't tarnish my credibility as a serious woman."

"There are a great many serious people who enjoy Rock and heavy metal. There are people who enjoy jazz. Not everyone listens only to a single kind of approved music."

He stood straight and looked at the wall as if he was seeing it for the first time. "This would make an interesting series! A spin-off from your Rock article!"

He turned back to Mab. "We could interview all sorts of people whose tastes vary... on the kinds of music... The ramifications of Sean's cover story has *Roots!*"

Sitting stony-faced, Mab observed, "I may become violently ill."

"I'll be in touch." Not waiting for her reply and completely bemused, Wally walked away, actually making it through the door unaided.

Amabel glared after him. Then out the window. Then at her desk. And there lay the envelope. "Read it," Wally had said. No way.

She couldn't eat lunch. She walked around the streets of L.A. on that lovely southern California February day. She didn't pay any attention to anything except the turmoil that was destroying not only her nervous system and appetite, but probably her brain cells as well.

How could she be such a victim? How had things gotten so out of control? Could she really bring herself to go to that stupid concert and write something comprehensible? She was a reporter. She was detached, an observer, a coolheaded recorder of fact. She could do anything.

And if she saw Sean Morant? After she snatched him bald, she would probably drag him to a veterinarian and have him neutered like any other repugnant dog.

When she finally returned to her office, the ticket envelope was still lying there on her desk. Grimly she picked it up, held it in her hand and tapped it on her other fingers. Why didn't she want to open it?

Did she think Tris would say, "Gotcha!"? He wouldn't. That wasn't his style. Anyone who could think up so risky and perfect a revenge wouldn't have to say anything.

The envelope was sealed. Wally said there was a note enclosed. From Jamie? More than likely. Jamie had probably thought of this whole tit-for-tat business, knowing it was money in the bank for his boy, Sean. It did smack of a devious, taking advantage of the situation, publicity man's calculation.

She ripped the envelope open, destroying it. There was no ticket. Another Viking trick? But she'd ripped apart the note, too. She lay it out, her hands trembling with her fury, and she read it.

It said:

"I'll pick you up at the hotel after your seminar. You'll find the concert in Fort Wayne very interesting. And something of a contrast to your Indianapolis experience.

"My aunt is looking forward to meeting you. You may discount her threat to mix you in with the pork in her homemade sausage.

"Simon Quint is my godfather.

"With all good wishes, Tristan Ezekiel Roald."

Whatever she had expected in the note, it hadn't been anything compared to his dictatorial, Viking communication. How *dare* he?

And that sneaky little threat to her job if she didn't cooperate! How perfectly nasty of him! So Simon Quint was his godfather? Who ever heard of a Viking having a godfather?

She was so steamed by then that she slammed out of the office, down the stairs, five flights, and out onto the street to walk for blocks.

True, comprehensible, organized thought didn't come for some time. Then finally her pride intruded. She would not let that man cause her to renege on her commitment to her job. She would go to Indiana. She would hold her head up and give her talk to the Women's Seminar. And she would go to the concert. She would. And she would give as fair an evaluation as she was capable of giving.

And that would be the end of this farce that had been forced so ridiculously upon her. Then she would be through with it and, with luck, she would never hear Sean Morant/Tristan Roald's name spoken again. Not in all the rest of her life.

She looked up, and around, and she had not the vaguest idea where she was. She found a storefront Mission and inquired, and they loaned her the money to get a cab back to her office. But the cab declined to come for her in that particular section of L.A.

She returned the money to the Mission and started out on foot. Two rather frightening men said they were her escorts and they followed her along, calling directions on occasion, and they left her when she finally recognized the landmarks and knew where she was. She still had to walk the rest of the way, back to the office, where it was quitting time.

However, *she* was no quitter. She would go to Fort Wayne. This must be some trial that God intended to use to help forge her character. She would prove she could handle anything. She gathered her things and ran out to catch her bus. She sat in a stupor, changed buses and went on home, walking up the last, character-building hill to her house.

Although determined to survive, she was very dispirited. B.S. Her life had been so pleasant Before Sean.

It would be pleasant again. She would win through this stupid mess, and she would prevail. And all that junk. She had the right stuff.

So she called Jamie and with some distraction she requested copies of the lyrics to be sung in Fort Wayne. If she was going to be there, it would be a help, she thought spitefully, if she understood what Sean was caterwauling about—if anything.

She received the sheaf of poems, and she was quite surprised to find Sean Morant had written them. Some dealt with serious concerns. Interesting. Interesting.

In Indiana, while February is always nasty, March can be very tricky. There have been eighteen-inch snows in

March. There have been ice storms that ruin the fruit trees and freeze the tulips and daffodils. February and March in Indiana give weathermen the willies. It's the season the natives walk around with their shoulders hunched, ready for whatever.

Being the woman she was, Amabel Clayton checked the extended weather forecast in Indiana and took along some of her southern California winter gear. A raincoat. A corduroy suit, a dressy dress that had enough polyester in it that it could be rolled and stuffed into a shoe and still look good, a couple of long-sleeved cotton blouses and some twill trousers.

She also packed a sweater vest, and unlined soft leather gloves. She took heels and tennis shoes. She was prepared for winter weather . . . in southern California.

At fifty degrees Fahrenheit, a capricious March wind at forty miles per hour produces a windchill of ten degrees. That's what it was when Amabel got off the plane in Indianapolis.

Indianapolis did surprise her. With a million people, it was quite a large city. And it was unique. Because there were people there with some foresight, the downtown had been preserved. The Circle was a gathering place, and events were geared to the Circle all year long. The ice rink was still in operation. It was cold.

Well, she was in a cab, and then in the hotel, so the weather didn't matter that much.

The women who gathered for the seminar came from the nine Great Lakes states. Amabel knew several of those attending, and some of those responsible for the organization were very efficient and most welcoming. It was one of Amabel's first experiences with a true feminist meeting.

It was excellent.

They shared ideas, suggestions and gave advice. They planned how to help themselves, how to communicate, how to cope. They were earnest businesswomen. It was exhilarating since it was sharing support and understanding.

But there was one jarring note. There was a session on how to have a feminist household. And it baffled Amabel why a woman would think a working man would want to live in one, any more than a working woman wants to live in a male-oriented household. Instead of male or female households there should be family households, teamwork. It wasn't hostility that should be taught, but cooperation.

The most shocking statement was, don't do anything for anyone who can do for himself. Alone that would be correct and would apply equally to anyone in the entire household. But when one woman asked, "My husband does all those things, am I being selfish?" The reply was, "Count your blessings."

The woman's husband was doing things for her that she could have done for herself. That wasn't wrong? It was only wrong if she was doing things for him that he could do for himself?

It was the only flaw in the logic of a serious, earnest, helpful meeting. Since one session didn't balance, it bothered Mab, the labeled man hater.

With tired feet walking in too-high heels down the long corridor, Mab was considering just that subject: men. And she was comforting herself that it wasn't a problem to trouble her.

She would never give up her job on the magazine for any man, and her routine was too strange to accommodate a relationship. Even if she was male, it wouldn't be the ideal job for a man who wanted a woman in his life. Reporters were better off single.

And a pair of male shoes under male trousers blocked her way. Men. She raised disgruntled eyes to pierce the stupid male who was setting up a hopeful flirtation, and she looked into the golden glinted brown eyes of what's his name. Sean or Tris or whatever he called himself today.

He smiled.

Even startled by the excitement that swept through her insides just at the sight of him, she managed to appear perfectly sober and very cool as she said, "You set me up."

"I've decided to marry you."

In disgust, she put both her hands on her hips exactly like an oil driller whose drill has broken off three thousand feet below the surface. She did an exact replica of such a man's deep, grim sigh as she tightened her lips, and she turned half away from The Cause as if there was no conceivable response to something that irritatingly stupid.

It was not a good beginning.

He grinned and asked, "Rough session?"

She didn't bother to reply.

"I figure we can get married quite soon, before the next tour. I'll be finishing up a six-city one that'll be done after Fort Wayne. Then there's a breather, and we can honeymoon."

She carefully spaced out the reasonable words as one would to a very dense person. "This is the second time we have met. Even without our quarrel, we are not friends. You are being typically Rocker Ridiculous. Under the circumstances, your speaking of anything as serious as marriage is an insult."

"You didn't tell my real name." He appeared to believe he'd explained it all as if completely. "You had the opportunity, but you resisted. Simon Quint said you wouldn't use it."

"It's nothing to my credit. I was excessively tempted. You pulled an unspeakable trick on me."

"I taught you a lesson." He was surprised she hadn't realized that and needed to be told, so he continued to instruct her. "Never believe what you read and only half of what you see." Then he added with a smile, "Simon Quint has fed me those kind of homilies since I could hold my eyes open right after birth."

"I interviewed those women."

"They gave prejudicial versions. I'm not a womanizer."

She scoffed.

"You and I were photographed coming from a hotel together."

She raised dangerously cautioning eyes to his.

He spread his arms innocently. "I just meant that great liberties could be taken in the speculation as to why we were there, walking out of the hotel together."

"Let me pass."

"I've come to fetch you to Fort Wayne."

"This is Thursday—the concert is not until tomorrow. I have other things to do." She gave him a killing look that should have dropped him in his tracks, right there in that hall.

"Good. I'll go with you."

"Do not interfere with me." But then her insides trembled at the very thought of his interference and such ramifications.

He replied gravely, "Oh, no."

"Your middle name is not Ezekiel."

He grinned. "I thought it would make you feel secure."

"Secure! Do you realize what kind of man he was?"

"Yes. It's suppertime. You'll feel better after you've eaten."

"I am not going anywhere with you." The words were as they were supposed to be, but her voice was rather faint. Unsure.

"Just here in the hotel dining room. You couldn't be safer. And I'll behave."

"No." She formed the word slowly as she watched his mouth.

"Then I won't behave. I'll gather you up and run down the stairs into the lobby and yell, 'Amabel Clayton's here! Call *US* magazine!' It would be sensational!"

He would.

"Just dinner," he coaxed.

"I'm very, very angry with you."

He shrugged. "I was madder'n hell with you, and if I'm willing to forgive you, then you must be equally forgiving. God says we must."

"I interviewed those women because I couldn't interview you."

"No excuses."

She charged, "You were deliberate."

"You weren't?"

She eyed him. Grudgingly she mentally conceded he had a couple of points. If she was going to have to ride two hours with him to Fort Wayne the next day, it would be a good opportunity to do a truly in-depth interview. "Will you allow me to write an interview?"

"With final copy approval."

Her blue eyes watched him as she shook her head in exasperation. "If I do get the interview, everyone will be sure I got it on my back." She looked aside, a bit sad.

"There's that, but you know you didn't."

"One of Quint's homilies has to be about sticks and stones..." She lifted blue eyes to him. "But words *can* hurt."

"Join the club." His husky voice was gentle. Then he told her, "You realize that, in giving you an interview, I'll have to do others?"

"It'll be good for your character."

He complained with impatience, "It takes so damned much time!"

She waited a while, and it was her body that forced the reply, "I'll meet you in the lobby." She knew she wasn't being obedient; she wanted to be with him again.

"I have the room next to yours."

"The hotel is packed, how did you manage that?"

"I made the reservation some time ago. I knew we'd want to be close."

"I'm not sure but what I should catch the next plane back to California, resign and find another position." She was serious. She felt on the verge of something important—but something very scary.

"To leave would be a coward's way. Your father would be ashamed of you."

He would, too. "I'll see you in the dining room." And she almost smiled.

She put on the purple silk, brushed her dark hair until it shone, then she added makeup a little more lavishly than usual. Her mind inquired why was she taking such pains to dress up for this stranger? She declined to search for a reason and coaxed her feet back into the heels. Then, ignoring their protests, she strode to the elevator and went down to the dining room.

She almost missed him since, as Tris Roald, he was so anonymous. She was beginning to think he'd stood her up, and disappointment had started to swamp her. But he was watching for her and came to her. They were seated by the maître d' and ordered.

Inanely she babbled, "You must eat out all the time."

"We seldom have the time to really enjoy leisurely meals. Especially on the road. There are so many details."

"Who's taking care of the details now, when you are here? Why aren't you in Fort Wayne?"

"The rest are covering for me while I fetch you."

"You make me sound like a stick."

He laughed. "No, you're assuredly no stick. And your eyes are so blue."

Impulsively she told him, "I was astounded you are Sean Morant."

"It astounds me, too. Who would ever believe I would be not only in this business but a success in it?"

"Then it's really serious if you lose your voice?"

"I am a frugal man. We are planning things carefully so the group doesn't suffer when we are finished. That time will come. Want the scoop?" He grinned at her.

"You are well thought of as a musician."

Very seriously he met her eyes. "I am a good man."

She couldn't misunderstand him. "You have to admit the circumstances suggested otherwise?" She sounded a little petulant, but surely not jealous?

"Perhaps."

"It was the relentlessness of you walking along with all those different women."

He added quickly, "—and you."

"I still think that was totally uncalled for."

"We're sitting here in Indianapolis and will soon be on our way to Fort Wayne. If I hadn't pulled that 'stunt' you'd be back out in California with no cause to be here."

"I was coming to Indianapolis anyway."

"But you're going on with me."

Her blue eyes widened. "Do you mean to imply that setup was calculated beyond simply getting back at me?"

"It was the first step of my plans for you. I half fell in love with you the first minute I laid eyes on you. I saw you in New York when Simon interviewed you for the job three years ago. I've read every one of your articles."

"Good grief."

"You don't believe me?"

"Not by any means."

"Then you're in for even greater shocks. Eat your dinner, you'll need your strength."

Four

They dined overlooking the atrium, the open entrance. The dining room was off the balcony, and they could watch as other people went about below on the ground floor, with its tiny shops, or as they walked along the balcony. He seated her, and they ordered.

As had happened when she was with him in California, her body reacted to his. She was there with him. He was just there by her elbow. If she reached out her hand she could actually touch him.

The thought of touching him made her a little restless. What would he do if she touched him? Probably knock her hand away. He'd set her up for that rotten picture.

For declared antagonists, Amabel thought they talked quite easily. That was a surprise, especially since she wasn't trying to get along with him. There wasn't any possibility for an interview, so she was herself. Well, somewhat *more* than herself for, having just been stimulated by the Women's Seminar, she didn't cater to him in any way.

"Indiana has strange weather." It was an immediate challenge.

"Spoken like Ezekiel's own issue."

"What's Ezekiel have to do with Indiana?"

"As I recall, that individual rejected the New England states. You've been east?"

"East of what?"

"Sorry, I forget you're West Coast and have a mental block about the East Coast."

Without a single qualm, she interrupted, "There was a reunion two years ago of all that Boston branch of the family. We went. It's strange to stand around in a mob of unknown people who are kin to you in some way, however vague."

With interest, he inquired, "Were you alienated?"

"They were very funny. Their humor surprised me."

He nodded. "The ability to laugh helps."

"I saw a PBS 'paper' on South American monkeys, and it showed them pulling the tails of parrots. Deliberately, to tease them. And the monkeys pulled a *python's* tail! Followed it along a branch, pulling its tail!"

"So you like to watch animals. There's a very special children's zoo in Fort Wayne."

"Do you hunt?" She watched him.

"On occasion."

She looked away as she shifted her body. "I see."

"How's the lamb?"

Her eyes widened as she gasped, "You beast."

And he laughed.

That caught her attention. He'd given no lecture, but he'd made his point and he'd been easy.

They explored mutual interests, which were another surprise. Her physical awareness of him intensified, and Mab found herself watching him as he ate. Except that he gave her no telling or sly glances, watching him was as erotic to her as the dinner scene in *Tom Jones*.

She watched Tris's hands, his mouth and his thickly lashed eyes as, in turn, he watched his food or drink...or he glanced at her.

She noted his discreet tongue. He gradually began to drive her body mad and to astonish her brain. He couldn't possibly know how he affected her.

Her brain said Tris ate just like any other ordinary human male. Her body yearned for his eyes to look at her in that manner, for his hands to touch and for his mouth...and tongue.

Quiverings stole along her nerve ends and excited obscure places that were very private.

This mind/body debate led to some odd pauses in her conversation as her brain was distracted in the effort to understand her body. During that process, her eyes clung to Tris's mouth or watched his hands almost mesmerized.

When she looked up, she saw that—in turn—he was watching her, with yellow fires smoldering in the brown, lash-shaded eyes. She swallowed and blushed, then blushed more deeply and lowered her eyes as he smiled an intense, soft smile.

He must be tired of mesmerized females. She probably bored him, she was so obvious. And she wasn't even a nubile teenage groupie. She was twenty-eight.

So? He was attractive. That was no excuse for her to be like every other stupid female and go berserk just because he was within reach. How embarrassing! And he'd caught her watching him like some loony.

Throughout the rest of the meal, her blush never entirely faded. As aware of herself as her body had managed, her brain could only be appalled. This was not the conduct of a professional woman.

Of course, calling a woman "professional" used to mean only one thing, her brain mused. And her body minutely squirmed in sensual response.

All of Tris's cells were riveted to Amabel. He tried not to stare. But his eyes refused to pay much attention to his command to be only briefly on her. He had trouble when she lifted her fork and took a bite into her mouth. Her lips parted to admit the bite, then closed over it, and he wanted his mouth to be the fork.

He was breathing shallowly, high in his chest. He tried not to move restlessly in the effort to ease his discomfort, but there wasn't any way to distract himself at the table.

He tried to think of something mundane, things to talk about that didn't become sensual images. Things which didn't fill his mind with brief, almost subliminal visions of her under that waterfall in Brazil, naked; or in that Danish field running toward him; or standing naked by him, on the parapet he remembered as he spoke of the view out over San Francisco's harbor.

He forced himself to discuss possibilities to solve the Ethiopian drought crisis and what must be done first when it abated. And he went on to the change coming in Ireland.

None of his distractions worked. He saw Mab in those places coping bravely, and he knew he needed to be with her, taking care of her, protecting her and making love with her.

Even in his bemusement, he realized all his imaginings were foolish flights of fancy. She didn't show any signs of being attracted to him. How could he have come so far in his awareness of her as an extremely desirable woman? Just seeing her as she'd come from his godfather's office that day, three years ago, had given him an interest in her, and as time had passed, her articles had kept him reminded of her.

Then the cover story she'd concocted of him and the variety of his acquaintances. He wasn't sure he'd been as offended as he appeared or if he'd simply seized the opportunity to contact her. It was a great excuse. It had worked. There they were, in Indianapolis, and they would be driving up to Fort Wayne the next day... together.

He lifted his spoon to taste the mouth-freshening, between-courses sherbet, and his eyes met hers. She was watching him in the most languorous manner, and it was marvelous that he didn't spoon the sherbet into his nose.

He lowered his eyes and tried to define her look. It didn't seem hostile. He was used to avid, almost maniacal women screeching and reaching. He'd lost track of interpreting female expressions. He lifted his eyes again, and she had paused as she stared at him so seriously, her cheeks were flushed. She hadn't had that much wine.

What if she was attracted? What if she was... willing? Their rooms were right next to each other. How convenient! But what if she was simply trying to figure out what the hell she was doing having dinner with a Rocker who had insulted her? One who had contrived to slap her down? He wished to God he hadn't. She didn't deserve such asinine conduct from any man.

She said, "The sherbet is excellent."

He realized they had been silent for some time. He smiled at her tenderly and replied, "Yes." His eyes rested on her pink cheeks. "Have you been outside since you came to Indianapolis?'' She could be sunburned or windburned with the varied Indiana weather.

"No. It's been very busy. At the seminar. It was well-organized. The hotel is so complete. There's no need to leave it." Because the explanation was so choppy and had to sound idiotic, she added, "You know."

His reply wasn't any better organized. "It's as warm as summer outside," he told her. "We should go out to the Lily Museum tomorrow. We'll steal the morning for ourselves. We need to drive to Fort Wayne in the early afternoon, but it would be nice to nose around a little and see something of Indianapolis. We should be outside while we can. There're storms predicted for this weekend."

"When do you have to be in Fort Wayne?" That was better—more to the point.

He smiled to share the ruefulness of his stolen time. "Two days ago."

"Maybe we should get up early and go on to Fort Wayne. It's a fair size city. I read up on it. There's a reconstructed fort, a children's zoo and several cathedrals that are special."

"I won't have time—" he began regretfully.

"I don't need anyone to hold my hand. I'm a grown woman. I can rent a car and go see those things alone...unless I can watch the preparations for the concert?"

Hastily, he promised, "Absolutely."

"Oh, well, then I'll do that. I do have a camera. It's a foolproof one."

"You wouldn't mind leaving early?"

She replied, "Not at all."

"Are you tired?"

She admitted, "It's been a long three days."

"How about just a little dancing?" He wanted to hold her because he was afraid she might balk at kissing him good-night. But if he held her while they danced, being in his arms wouldn't be as strange, and she might allow him to hug her good-night and perhaps he could get a kiss in.

He smiled. He hadn't plotted like this since he was seventeen. He said offhandedly, "Just a couple of dances. It would be nice to see if I still remember how."

She retorted, "I didn't bring my army boots."

"Oh ye of little faith."

"Another of Simon's sayings?"

He nodded. "When he doesn't see me for a while, they pile up and he writes them to me in stern notes."

"He has been very kind to me."

"He's in New York, and you're in California." Tris frowned. "What do you mean he's been 'very kind' to you?"

"He lets me alone to write as I want to."

Pretending hostility, he frowned darkly at her. "Even your cover on me?"

"The article surprised Mr. Quint. He said that you—" she tilted her head as she remembered the words "—are deeper, wider and more complex ... than I made you appear. I thought that was interesting at the time. I didn't know then that he was your godfather."

"He never married. He was very moved that my parents would ask him to be my godfather. He takes the role seriously." He lifted his eyes to hers.

"What made you go into a Rock band? The more I know you, the more surprising it is. Eddie Van Halen's another who surprises me. He is a remarkable musician, and apparently an awesome guitarist."

"You've been researching."

"Of course. Jamie gave me the lyrics of the songs you're using on this tour. Your words are very moving. And—"

"Thank you."

"Don't be so sweetly hasty. I was beginning to say that your view of women is primitive. We need to discuss women's rights."

"Hasn't that been beaten to death? I'd think, by now, everybody's well-informed as to the way women want to be treated."

"Equally."

He smiled and bit his lower lip to keep from saying something completely wicked. She saw that and she knew it was so! And blast if she didn't laugh! How irritating of her.

It was her body that was interfering; it *knew* how it wanted a man to treat her. But the appalling thing was, Mab never before had had that interference from her body's hungers. To be in a perfectly serious discussion, and to have her brain overridden by a salacious body? It was unnerving.

She tried to get out of going dancing. She didn't think she should allow her body that privilege of being held by this particular man. He unsettled her. Unsettled? He about had her standing on her ear!

He countered her objection. "The problem is, if we don't go dancing tonight, I might not get to for years. This is a complete fluke. I'm playing hooky. The guys are covering for me. And they'll say, 'What all did you do?' And I'll say, 'We went to dinner,' and they'll say, 'And?' And I'll be forced to say, 'That's all.'"

"And that will be all." She said it quite staunchly.

"But then they'll think..." He looked distressed as he opened his hands, discreetly trying to explain. "They'll think we couldn't wait to go up to bed and make love."

She gasped indignantly. Surely it was indignation?

He rushed on. "The women around Rock stars aren't subtle. Those kind of women are the only kind the band's been around lately. They don't understand normal courting. If I can say we went dancing—with all honesty, since I would have to be telling the truth—then they might have doubts. They are a little like fish realizing all is not water.

"But if I lied about us dancing, and even if you just went on to your room—alone—then they'd feel sure I was lying. They would immediately jump to the erroneous conclusion that we spent the night in unrestrained passion."

Blushing, she sat straight in shock, for her body had discarded dancing and was clamoring for his band's version to the evening's end. Her mouth had to try several times for something suitable to say besides sputtering protests. She finally managed, "We'll go dancing."

"Oh, good. I hate to lie. Simon says to thine own self be true, and he's right as always." But instead of looking sober as he should have with that line, his eyes glinted golden lights and his mouth couldn't quite not smile.

So he was going to hold her. He was going to dance with her and hold her against him. They both shivered with the thought. But his mind was involved with her softness, while she was mesmerized by his strength.

He inquired of the waiter and found that a lounge, there in the hotel, had dancing during the weeknights. It was just down the balcony from the dining room, and it was called the Well House.

* * *

There is speculation that sex is ninety percent brain
and only ten percent body hunger. It would be interesting to see the people who came to that conclusion. Of
course, Amabel had been convinced of the ninety/ten
ratio before that fateful night.

Her body had already intruded like a hungry primitive, lusting after Tris. Her entire sensory system was
aware of every move he made, and only the harsh, brain
command—that she was to keep her hands locked together—kept her from touching him, stroking, petting.
It was just a good thing she had such control.

But it was her brain that was in control then. If her
brain had been the interested part, that mythical ninety
percent, she would have laid him out under the table in
a disgraceful display. But her brain was in steely control
over her avariciously sensual body. She could handle the
situation.

She congratulated herself too quickly. As soon as his
arms were around her, in the brief hesitation to assimi-
late the beat of the music, she was lost. Then he moved
her backward with great skill in the aggressive, male
dominance of the dance. Her last fragment of cohesive
thought was that he hadn't forgotten a thing.

The alleged ten percent of her body turned her brain
off so that it slid into a corner, helpless and totally use-
less. Her body was then free of restriction as she relished being against his. Her cells were drunk with the
pleasure of it. The difference of it. The newness of it.

There was no control at all. It was as if her excited,
silly nerves all giggled in almost hysterical excitement
and nudged each other. She had to gasp and press
against him, as erotic feelings went skittering through
her body.

She was so obviously physically aware of him that he was quite surprised. He was unresisting and taking full advantage of it but still delightedly surprised. And he cooperated quite nicely. He held her closely. He savored the feel of her plastered against him.

Music was his soul. He felt it, related to it, responded. That, coupled with her surrender, was formidable. He moved his wide-spread hand on her back, he made his dance steps slower, more erotic; and she followed blindly, like a sheep after a Judas goat.

At one point, her brain battered her conscience with guilt and training, so that she leaned a weakly supported head back and looked up at Tris with heavy eyes as she lay against him. Her languid hand brushed a strand of hair from her forehead and she said with slowly moving lips, "I believe I had too much wine."

He laughed, genuinely amused. She was looking for excuses to explain her behavior! She'd had several sips of wine from one small glass. He knew because he'd used all sorts of tricks to get her to drink more and hadn't been successful.

She was drunk, all right. With desire. For *him*. What more powerful aphrodisiac is there for a man? A desirable woman, he craved, who was helpless in her need for him. He could have her. He could take her up to his room, and she would let him make sweet, tender love to her.

He almost crushed her boneless body as he hugged her in the excuse of a turn in their steps. And he allowed his senses the pleasure of the possibility that had turned into assurance. She would.

And she would have. But when they went to their rooms, he took her to her door, unlocked it and then he kissed her for the first time. It was like being drugged with a magical wizard's formula, for the sensations were that marvelous.

Tris's hands shook and his breaths trembled. She was malleable, his for the taking. And he almost could not resist. He allowed himself the feel of her softness. His hands moved and treasured. His mouth caressed. But he released her.

That did confuse her. She blinked, trying to understand as he turned her and patted her bottom. He said he'd waken her very early, and she needed her sleep. Then he closed the door behind her.

She was still standing there in her vacant room, a lump of roiling need, when he tapped on the door. He'd been teasing! She opened the door, fumbling with the dumb mechanism, and her face was so welcoming that he groaned.

He kissed her eager mouth, held her reaching hands and told her to put on the chain. "Do you understand?"

She nodded; her smile faltered and her eyes looked hurt.

"We'll be together tomorrow."

"Yes."

"We do need to sleep. It's late. The concert is tomorrow."

"Yes."

"Good night, Amabel."

"Yes." She was in something of a stupor.

"Lock the door and put on the chain."

"Yes."

"I would like to make love with you. We'll talk about it."

She frowned, trying to figure out why any talk was needed.

"Lock the door—"

A little irritated, she completed it, "—and put on the chain."

She was functioning. He kissed her quickly and closed the door. But he stood there and listened to her fumbling with the lock; then she struggled with the chain.

Having verified she had obeyed, Tris took his complaining, thwarted body to a cold shower and to bed. He didn't want a one-night stand with her. And if he had to drive her crazy with wanting him to really get her attention, then he would do that.

In her room, Mab faced the fact that she had wanted to be seduced by Tris Roald, and she was more than a little ashamed. She didn't really know him. One afternoon in California, one dinner and dancing in Indianapolis and a lot of videotapes was all she knew of him. All the videotapes in the world did not a friendship make—or an affair.

Was she really just like everyone else? Susceptible just because a devastating man might be willing? Surely not. Where was her control? How dare the experts say sex was all mental, giving her the false sense of security that her mind was in control!

If it hadn't been for Tris, she would have gone to bed with him, and—with her luck—gotten pregnant. She was so sure she'd never be tempted that she simply was not prepared for sex.

She, too, took a long cold shower, thinking that—really—she should be grateful he was cool enough to call a halt to her blind passion. She did think that, but she wasn't all that grateful. Finally she went to bed and after a while, she slept.

* * *

She was still a little disgruntled with Tris the next
morning. Conversely that amused him, and he was very
sweet to her.

That made her want to hit him with her omelet. She
looked at him with steely blue eyes that were narrowed
as she "saw" him sitting there decorated with her Span-
ish omelet.

He glanced up and smiled at her.

She gave him a quelling glare before she went back to
eating. She mumbled only brief replies to his cheerful
attempts at conversation. She couldn't understand why
he should be so... jaunty that morning.

The first time she'd ever considered a tumble, and
he'd ignored all the obvious signals of her willingness.
Was she so inept? Or maybe he just teased and enjoyed
frustrating women? She'd thought men were easy.

A part of her ill temper was embarrassment. She'd
offered herself so obviously and had been declined. At
least he hadn't put one hand on her chest and shoved her
off him. But she'd been very blatant, her revived mind
reminded her. Unladylike. Loose. Surely not loose?
Loose.

Again fully in control, her mind mentioned that
probably all the people who'd been in the lounge last
night had noticed her behavior and been appalled that a
woman would act in such a way, in public with a man.
Or they had sniggered. Her pale cheeks pinked up and
she kept her eyes on her plate.

He wondered if she was an innocent. At what...
twenty-five? He asked, "How old are you?"

She'd been told she looked young. Surely he didn't
think she was a San Quentin Quail? "I'm twenty-eight."

"I'm thirty-six." He smiled tenderly at her.

Obviously he was old enough and so was she, so what was his problem? Maybe he had one of the horrendous diseases? Or did he think *she* did? How dare he?

He was the Rocker. He was the one women clawed at and fought over. She ought to have known better than to offer herself. He was probably worn-out. Depleted. Incapable.

She shot a glance at him and intercepted a very amused look. He didn't look depleted.

He talked to her and treated her as if she was fragile crystal. He touched her, and she flinched away because her reaction to his touch was so electric. His husky voice was gentle and his words were kind. He ignored what a jenny she was making of herself and acted as if she was being perfectly normal.

When his rental car was delivered from the parking garage, she added her Fort Wayne made Vera Bradley quilted cloth luggage to his bags in the trunk. She was riding into the sunrise with a Rocker!

Mab shook her head and reminded herself quite succinctly that she was on an assignment. There was no room for her to be this obtuse. She was a professional.

In a great, world-rocking concession, Tris asked, "Would you like to drive?"

"No, thank you," she replied shortly.

"As an equal-righted woman?"

She wasn't sure she could wrest her attention from him to attend to the mechanics of driving. "I'd rather not."

"No...real problem." He managed to hide his relief.

Through the muggy, fooled, summerlike March day, they drove north on Meridian to Highway 465. From the corners of her eyes, she watched his hands on the wheel and how his thigh flinched as he drove. He drove skillfully.

Their silence was awkward. Finally as they turned north on Interstate 69, she got out her pad and pen and asked with brisk efficiency, "How can you, as famous and popular as you are, go about undetected?"

She was so interesting to him. She was so precious. Everything she did charmed him. She sat there in her prim blouse and sweater vest with her twill trousers and tennis shoes. Her lips were thinned down prissily so that he wanted to stop the car and kiss them soft and swollen with passion. He smiled.

"Does it bother you to talk? I know your vocal cords are giving you problems."

"Only with singing. I began singing with the band in college, and I had no voice training. We hit the video fever at exactly the right time, and two songs from our first album went to the top of the charts and stayed there. It was pure, unadulterated luck.

"We caught on and simply rode the wave for however long it would last. We had no idea we'd stay there. Singing is like everything else. You can just have at it, and do it—but if you aren't trained correctly, you can louse up.

"It's like boxing, or tennis, or any physical thing. You need to know how to protect yourself. I've harmed my voice by singing, untrained."

"Do you choose not to answer the first question?" she inquired coolly.

"How do I go around unrecognized? I'm not sure. I'm not a good-looking man. I'm quite ordinary." He'd said so on occasion, to such emotional contradiction, that it tickled his funny bone when she allowed him to say it without even a murmur of rebuttal.

He explained, "I believe it must be like the story of Marilyn Monroe. She was in Central Park and her friend was astonished she could walk along without being recognized.

"Marilyn said it was because she wasn't using her movie-star personality. Her friend didn't believe it. Marilyn said to watch, and before the friend's eyes Marilyn turned into a 'personality' and she was swamped with people who immediately recognized her."

He explained, "I don't feel like a Rock Star off the stage. I'm an ordinary man. I don't expect to be recognized. I don't know if there's any proof to Marilyn's premise, even though she apparently proved it." He drove silently for a minute, then added, "Offstage I don't dress like a Rocker. I dress like Tris Roald. My hair is neat. My clothes are anonymously like everyone else's. My attitude is different from Sean Morant's. He's a different man."

"How do you feel when you're Sean Morant?"

"If you're suggesting a Dr. Jekyll and Mr. Hyde personality split, I'm not aware of a schism. It's simply that onstage I am a performer. Offstage I am not."

"Have you ever taken drugs?"

"No. Long ago, Simon Quint had me talk to a man who is a friend of his. A psychiatrist who experimented with drugs in the sixties, before the danger was understood. He is now salvaging those smart enough to realize the disaster of it. The doctor told me exactly what those substances do to the body, the brain, to the organs, and to the children born who must contend with that. I was impressed.

"None of the band has touched the stuff. I had the doctor talk to them." He looked briefly out across the rolling Indiana countryside. "We're good musicians in our band, and we get along together very well. We communicate. We're loyal Americans, however critical. We are human, we tell of lives and hopes and dreams. We're troubadours."

"No burn-out?"

"I believe the time is coming when we'll split. Tours are exhilarating. But they are exhausting. Our interests are widening. We may do some film scoring. I find moods of music fascinating."

"How do you deal with tension, the pressures?"

"We are fortunate that we can cope. We are like any other men in high-pressure jobs. Some make it, some bend and some break. We make it—bending now and again." He gave her a brief glance as he smiled.

As they drove along, the two hours it took to get to Fort Wayne, they went on talking. Amabel became involved with Tris. She began to know him. She was drawn to him. And it wasn't just her mindless body that was attracted.

He told her about his aunt who lived in Whitney County on a farm, west of Fort Wayne, and he told of visiting Indiana when he was a child, about his cousins and the things they did. He was funny, and he was nice. He was a good man, just as he said he was.

Five

From I-69, Tris and Amabel took the exit to Highway 24 into Fort Wayne. The charming city was set at the convergence of three rivers and had celebrated its bicentennial in 1994. Long ago it had been Miami Indian territory.

Now not quite two hundred thousand people lived there. It had its center city, and sprawling malls and suburbs. They had a remarkable number of good citizens who worked hard for the preservation of such a fine city.

And there were people who found solutions to places that were deteriorating or were abandoned. They watched to help where they could. And it was mostly offered help with a good many donated hours.

With March, the tall trees were still bare. The colorful spring flowers were a treat for the sight of them. The yards were neat.

Following directions, Tris drove through the streets of reclaimed old houses in the west-central part of the city. Their route to the coliseum went from Jefferson Street, to Clinton, to Spy Run with its bicycle path along the riverside, to Parnell. As predicted, there was the coliseum.

They left the car in the immense parking lot and walked toward the building.

By then, Mab had sat next to Tris for several hours, at breakfast and traveling in the car, but this was only the second time she'd walked beside him. There were no photographers.

It bemused her to feel that it was natural to stride along with him. A pair. That's what they were…a pair.

Did he feel that? How could he feel any differently walking along with her? In the pictures she'd gathered for the *Root's* cover, he'd walked beside all those other women, bored, in step.

She slid a glance up and saw that he was watching her. He didn't look bored. The sweep of feeling that slid through her caused her to stumble. It probably crossed her eyes and set her hair on end, too.

Tris caught her arm, then held it and slowed his stride. He hadn't been walking too quickly for her. She was perfectly capable of walking with a reasonable stride. Unless he was along. They then strolled, almost indolently, and she relished being beside him. It was as if they really were a pair.

They entered the coliseum's maze of ramps and openings and walked to the oval center floor, which was used for all sorts of meetings, gatherings, games and concerts. There was a good deal of activity, as the preparations for the night's concert progressed.

There were calls of direction and laughter. Someone was whistling cheerfully, very unselfconscious about doing so, as he walked along carrying a shoulder's burden of cables. But no one appeared to be idle.

Tris's publicist, Jamie Milrose, was the first familiar person Amabel saw, among the fifty some odd, purposeful workers on the arena floor. Jamie was in jeans and casual shirt with his sleeves rolled up.

Jamie's eyes came to Mab, and he watched only her as she and Tris came across the floor. Someone called to Tris, but with a gesture of delay, Tris gave a surprised greeting to Jamie. "Well, hello, Jamie, problems?"

"None at all," Jamie responded unsmilingly. "I just thought it time to check in on what goes on." That could mean anything.

Tris laughed. "You're due a thrilling time. We'll keep you busy."

"I am already. I have interviews lined up." Tris's eyes came to Jamie's as he frowned, but Jamie went on: "I figured Mab would have—weaseled—an interview out of you by now, and that leaves you open to the entire field. We've even managed an interview with a reporter from South Side High School, who is pacing with undue excitement."

Tris frowned and pulled his mouth down. "Ah, Jamie. You could have put them off?"

"Not and kept my soul clean." And he gave them both a level look.

"So be it." Tris excused himself to Amabel and went to the person who was waiting for some decision from Tris.

Amabel stood where Tris left her, and Jamie moved closer to her as he said, "Well, well, well." He didn't smile, his voice was low as if he told a secret and his eyes narrowed a little as he flicked them over her with stern censure. This was done by the man who had coaxed her to go to his place in Big Sur.

She bristled and gave him a cool look. "Hello, Jamie."

"You're with Sean." It was not a question but a blunt statement of fact.

She didn't respond but commented instead, "Are you helping with the setup?"

"I'm not a Roadie." He discarded that with a flick of his hand and asked, "You with Sean?"

"I walked in with him." That was a nice, evasive reply.

Jamie wouldn't leave it. "I heard he went down to Indy to fetch you. Are you with him?"

"Why?" Mab slid her glance over to him, very much like a woman had done to her when the question Mab had asked was none of her business. That's how Mab felt now with Jamie.

His voice stern and adult, he told her, "I need to know."

"Ask him."

Jamie growled, "He won't tell me."

She smiled a little.

He tilted his head back until his eyes were slits. "Mab the man hater? The unique woman? Just like any other? How disillusioning." He drew the word out with slow disdain.

Amabel looked around the arenalike floor, then up at its empty seats, rising row on row from a three-foot railing that began a good six feet or more above the floor. "I suppose it's like anything else." She opened out her hands, and she could have been indicating life or the coliseum, as she deliberately paused before she continued, "But they will be ready in time."

She was underlining the fact that she was ignoring his question. "I remember the first time I was in charge of a volunteer stage crew. I was the newest member, of course, and I *knew* on opening night the curtain would rise on a littered, incomplete stage. I had a blinding headache for a month." She smiled again quite nicely.

Jamie's voice roughened. "I had thought I would have you."

"As I recall—" she was quite cool "—your invitations were only for weekends at Big Sur."

"You're forgetting the rest. Are you sleeping with him?"

Her nostril-flare of indignation owed quite a bit to how close she'd come to it.

But her indignant reaction calmed Jamie. "Fort Wayne is my home," he said softly. "Will you come meet my family?"

"There won't be time. I leave first thing in the morning."

"I'll take you to the airport. It's 'way-the-hell, diagonally across town."

"No," said Tris's voice as, undetected in their concentration, he came up to them from behind Jamie. "I'm taking her." He didn't mention where or how.

He passed Jamie to stand beside Mab, and his fingers closed possessively on her elbow. It was the least thing he could do that indicated she was his, without intruding on her belief that she was still her own woman. He smiled at Jamie. It was a slow, quiet smile that was dangerous.

By then, all three were irritated. She most of all. The two men were faced off over her like dogs over a bone.

And her irritation came because Tris's fingers on her elbow had set off sensual shock waves that reverberated up her arm, into her nipples and down into her stomach. The feeling he had triggered was like a fingernail drawn softly up the center of her insides.

Why him? Why this Tris Roald/Sean Morant? Other men had been near to her, touched her arm, and there had never been this body reaction to *any* of them! Why could Tris's touch evoke such a response in her? Sex. How shocking!

Each of the three was aware of the tension which had nothing to do with the coming concert. It was, by then, midmorning. To break the spell of antagonism, they shifted their feet as they looked around. And they saw the caterer's replenishing crew leaving with trays of dirty dishes.

Without any discussion, they took advantage of the array of catered food and drink set up in one of the conference rooms along the outside of the circling lower hall.

The promoter had a caterer on hand the entire time. The available smorgasbord began with the first arrival of the Roadies, whether it was the night before or that morning.

There was a constant supply of food and a variety of soft drinks, for however long it would take to set up before the performance, to the last of the dismantling. The selection was wide, the food well prepared, and the three sampled with interest.

Jamie drifted away first, then Tris was consulted and Mab listened. Tris spoke quietly. He was courteous with his replies. If he disagreed, he wasn't arbitrary but made certain his reasons were understood, and he bent if the other's reasoning was better. He listened.

Mab noted all that, and how people looked at him, the way they liked Tris. How easy they felt with him. This was no "star;" this was a businessman. And Mab watched, but not as a reporter. She was judging him as a man.

Tris was taken away for the interviews Jamie had lined up. They were set up in the dressing rooms, which were within twenty feet from the back of the stage.

Two reporters, who had a cameraman along, questioned him for their *Journal Gazette* column. Tris didn't mention that, for one brief afternoon out on the West Coast, he had been their colleague.

For the time of the interviews, Mab was left to wander around, take pictures with her simple little no-fail purse camera, ask questions and watch. Any skilled person is fascinating. From a man on a dock who fillets fish, to a wrecking crew's unexpected planning and talent, to a mother who separates siblings. Or a lawyer who tries a case, or a doctor who operates, all are expected to be skilled.

But there are all the others who have talent in what they do. Those whose practiced movements are poetry, from a lineman on a pole, to a cement man who lays a walk, to the driver who backs a semi into a slot that fits almost too closely.

It was as fascinating for Mab to see the men and women in the coliseum as they skillfully prepared for so brief a performance. Each time, with each concert, in each different place, all of it had to be done, then moved to be re-done and done again and done correctly. They were like cooks, or dishwashers, or mothers picking up toys from the living room floor.

In the printed handouts from Jamie, concerning Sean Morant, Mab had read his praise for his Roadies. And now, observing the Roadies at work, she understood their contribution to the concert. Their vital contribution. And she could understand how they would feel a very necessary part of it.

In her questioning of the coliseum PR rep, Amabel learned the Memorial Coliseum, there in Fort Wayne, holds ten thousand people. "By actual count," her informant said, "it is nine thousand nine hundred ninety-*eight.*"

"Now why the two less than ten thousand?" Amabel grinned.

"The number is dictated by the Fire Marshal."

And Amabel asked, "With the great crowds in other parts of the country, it surprises me the big groups come for such a relatively small crowd."

"Well, it's a cozy place to a Rock group. The feedback from the crowd is more one-on-one, even though one of the 'one's' is almost ten thousand. The groups like to come here. People come to the events at the coliseum from a hundred miles around from the Indiana and Ohio countryside.

"An interesting thing of it, there at the Rock concerts, the crowds are primarily affluent teenagers. In other places you see adults and young adults. But in Fort Wayne, the crowds at the Rock concerts are made up mostly of teenagers, with a few younger, a number older and a sprinkling of adults."

"That is a surprise."

"It's a nice place to have a concert for the fans." The man looked around with a pleased glance. "It's nice for the groups who perform. The place lends a more intimate, involved feeling and the crowd appreciates the fact the bands come here."

"Do you ever have any trouble? How about drugs or drinking?"

"The overwhelming majority are well behaved." He gestured. "Cheerful participants in an event. There are those few who try the security by smuggling in booze or grass, but there aren't very many now—only about fifty in the almost ten thousand—and those who are that stupid are generally caught in the funnelling of the crowd as they come inside."

A wooden floor had been laid over the Komets' ice hockey rink, and the stage was erected. Since Tris's group was using the coliseum's stage, the road crew numbered only twenty-seven, and they hired twenty local union people to help set up. Electrical cables appeared like a peddler's box of fishing worms. And no one seemed especially harried.

With the variety of her interviews, Mab had learned—by watching—that there is a way people move when they know they must pace themselves in order to last. People who must walk a long way, walk at an almost regal pace.

And people who have a staggering amount of work to do, in order for everything to be ready for a performance, appear to move inordinately slow to the frantic uninitiated—who are generally in charge. But it is the same pacing. Slow but steady. As Mab had learned, it still wins races, and that way no one is hurt and there are fewer mistakes.

Had the group brought their own stage—as do some performers—they would have had seventy-five Roadies plus forty hired locals. They would have worked all the previous night.

Tris's crew of twenty-seven had arrived in town the night before and had been working, with the additional twenty local people, at the coliseum since seven that morning.

Besides erecting the in-house stage, the roadies would be responsible for the tuning of the instruments, the placing of lights and testing the sound equipment.

During the concert, they would man the lights and do the sound mix. It was a complicated business. A little like astronauts, with their awesome backup of skilled people, who take nothing from the skills of those "on-stage."

So far, Mab had been with Tris as Tris Roald. She'd only seen videos of him as Sean Morant. But as the day progressed, she saw the beginnings in Tris of Sean Morant, and it was an amazing metamorphosis.

Before her eyes, he was turning into someone unknown to her. He was becoming the personality of the videos. As a man, he was assured and in control. But now—in addition—he was becoming the performer. A public man.

She had discreetly watched as one woman interviewed Sean Morant for Fort Wayne's Channel 21. She was another professional, concise and prepared. Another skill to appreciate. Mab listened to the easy chatter between the members of the group who slid into the dressing room to share the interviews to help save Sean Morant's voice.

Being a reporter, Mab naturally noticed the people who paused to witness the interviews. And she watched the women's faces as they watched Sean Morant. Then she considered the men.

It was exactly as she'd witnessed with Sean Morant's videos. He was the ideal lover to the women. A sexual man. But with the men, he was a born leader. A man for men to join. To follow.

How did he do that? With curiosity, Mab studied Sean. He was relaxed. He didn't need to dominate the interview. He was amused. There was the feeling that he didn't really believe he was actually there and a target for attention.

While there was that modesty, however, there was no slurring of his talent. His musical abilities were a gift. One he could share. How we need our heros. What a burden it is to be one.

With the success of Bob Geldof's first LIVE AID, the interviewers talked about the annual worldwide Rock concert for funding to alleviate world hunger. The good that came of such effort. The staggering amounts of money, and the control guards that were instigated against greedy fingers.

Tris's group talked about the fun of meeting so many others like themselves. How interesting it was that the superstars could be just like the rest of us. The mega-stars were thrilled in turn to meet their own idols. And yet again, there was the verbal bow to the work of all those others who made it all work and who weren't ever seen on camera.

Mab watched a stranger named Tris whom she had begun to know, or thought she had, and he was some-one else. Someone who, as Simon Quint had said, was...wider, deeper and more complex than she could know.

In spite of the activity still going on around her in the afternoon, Mab lined up four folding chairs. She was dressed in the twill slacks, shirt and sweater vest. She had her all-weather coat for a cover, and she stretched out on her contrived bed, there at the cool edge of the performing pit. The air of the wood-covered ice creeped up to chill them all, but she slept heavily.

Jamie stopped once to stand solemnly and stare at her sleeping form. It was then Tris managed to come along. Quite deliberately, Tris rearranged Amabel's lined raincoat around her more closely before he added his own jacket over her.

Having done that, he went busily off, as if he hadn't noticed Jamie standing there. It amused Tris that he hadn't been able to resist marking his territory. But then, being blatant could avoid any misunderstanding.

Tris was covering her up again when she wakened. The sounds came into her consciousness first. A board dropped with its echo. There was the sound of a hammer. Someone calling. She opened her eyes as Tris sat on his heels by her and smiled.

He was Tris, whose presence set off such remarkable reactions inside her body. She felt the surge of desire as she found his eyes looking into hers. She licked her lips and blinked, foolishly thinking that would distract her from her reaction to him. She commanded an indifferent yawn, and she did a passingly good job of it.

His chuckle was deliciously low in his raspy throat. "What a lazy woman you are," he scolded her intimately, as if he had that right. "Lying around, doing nothing, when we've a performance this very night."

Feeling capable of it, she looked up into his face, so close to hers. So intimately close in that big, busy place, she then replied seriously, "I've eaten my full share of the catered food."

"Oh, I hadn't realized you were that diligent. I owe you an apology."

"Yes."

The husky words came then, "Are you going to kiss me for luck?"

The very thought made her toes curl. Sensations slid up the insides of her thighs to circle lazily and stretch out fully inside her body, touching all sorts of places that responded shamelessly.

The feeling even involved the undersides of her arms and, as she contemplated that, she noted her ears were affected and that her scalp tingled.

All the reaction was because Tris was there by her, watching her? Incredible. Again she had to lick her lips before she could reply, "Do you always have some handy female around to perform that duty?"

"Not until now."

"Balderdash."

He laughed over the word. "Where did you find...balderdash?" He said it as if he tasted the word.

"My grandmother. She could string it out to be so tellingly disgusted or unbelieving."

Tris replied readily enough, "I have a surprise for you this evening. I have a song for you."

"A song?"

"Just for you."

"Pish and tosh." She wasn't at all impressed—that she could show. She scoffed, "You're probably just like George Gershwin who had a song he kept unpublished. And he secretly played it for every woman he liked as 'her song'—until the next woman came along. I know that's true, because I saw it in a movie and movies don't ever lie."

"I just wrote this one." Then he inquired, in after-thought, "Pish and tosh?"

"An excellent reply," she assured him. "For people who argue, it stops them dead in their tracks, every time.

There is simply no topper. It worked for my grand-mother."

His eyes were almost hidden by his lashes. But the yellow fires were there. He said, "Tomorrow we have to go by to see my aunt on our way back to Indy."

"Why go back to Indianapolis?" she asked quite logically. "There is a perfectly good, working airport here, and planes fly in and out all day and half the night."

"We'll have a direct flight from Indianapolis. And I can't be here and not go to my aunt's. They'll all be at the concert tonight. You'll sit with them, but we'll still have to go see them tomorrow. Okay?"

"No need for me." She was uncomfortable about it.

"They wouldn't understand if you didn't go with me." He was reasonable. "And you couldn't wait outside, in the car in the barnyard, while I visited with them. They would think you were strange. Anyway, you'd miss the fun." He slyly added the clincher, "It'll give you another facet of Sean Morant for your article."

"That's true."

"But it's mostly because they are such nice people." With clear pictures of them all in his mind, he couldn't resist adding, "You'll be delighted with their respect and admiration for me, those simple, plain country folk." He licked his lips and glanced aside so she didn't see the humor.

He sighed with some talent for drama. "I am glad you're not normally a foul-mouthed woman. My aunt is death on swearing."

"So's my dad. That's how I became involved with my grandmother's balderdash and pish and tosh."

"Ummm," he acknowledged her words with the sound before he continued. "It is a little difficult to talk to these relatives of mine. I won't be there to introduce subjects tonight. How much do you know about sow bellies, corn futures and soil drainage?''

"Not a whole lot," she admitted.

"Well." He was doubtful. "I suppose you could talk about me." And he gave her a sweet look.

She lay there and closed her eyes as she hit her forehead with the palm of her hand. "You've been setting me up again...right?" She looked at him, very disgusted.

"Would I do that?" He was appalled by the idea. Indignant. "You'll see." And his wicked, wicked smile fooled her.

He leaned quickly and kissed her open mouth before she knew what he was up to, wreaking complete havoc on her nervous system, her dignity, and ruining the purpose of her knees. Then he swatted her hip, took her hand and expected her to get to her feet! "Go straighten yourself out and wash your hands—we have to eat again."

Delaying actual movement, while she tried for body coordination after such a kiss, she asked in a credible mumble, "How can you eat so much and still be slender?" And she was impressed her words made some sort of sense.

"Men aren't 'slender,'" he said in disgusted protest. "They're 'fit.' We work our tails off for a concert. We need food. The caterer has brought in a whole new supply. You'll be pleased with the selection. Hop! I'll meet you in the hall between the rest rooms."

As he had claimed, there was a remarkable selection of food. Of appetizers, soups, meats, vegetables, fruits and desserts. She took a smorgasbord of taste bites. He drank some clear, unsalted beef broth and had a dish of sherbet.

Sitting next to him, she felt like a pig with her loaded plate. "I thought you were hungry."

"We've eaten all day. I'll eat again after the show. I have stage fright, and I can only handle the broth and some sherbet. I've found that out through trial and impressive error."

"You have *stage fright?*" She had trouble believing it.

"The pitch begins to rise pretty soon. The day's restlessness mounts, and the closer to time for the performance, the worse it gets. The majority of public performers have the problem." He shook his head. "It's ridiculous. Once onstage, it's a high you wouldn't believe.

"The feedback from the audience is such a—a—it's phenomenal. I've heard there is one star who records just the applause from appearances and, in times of depression, plays the records to feel and absorb the approval. People are fragile."

"If you are serious about quitting, will you be able to give it up?"

"I'll miss it. No question. But I'll make another life. This isn't primary for me. I get satisfaction from other sources. And I realize how fortunate I am that's so."

And again she heard Simon Quint's words that Tris was more of a man than she'd ever suspected, but she was beginning to understand.

Six

At thirty-six, Sean Morant was riding on the crest of the crowded Rock scene. There were those venerable ones, in their forties, who were the legends. If Elvis was still alive, he would have moved into his sixties. Would the time come when there were Rock treasures in their eighties, as there are now in jazz?

The passage of time, Tris drolly reported, had been brought succinctly to his attention when a junior—in high school—pleaded to have his baby "Before it's too late." That had made him blink. Too late? *At thirty-six?* Age, like beauty or evil, is in the eyes of the beholder. And Tris laughed.

"What will you wear tonight?" Mab asked the feminine question.

Tris smiled quickly. "Would you like to choose? The Roadies brought in the wardrobe. We all wear whatever we want to," he explained to Amabel. "Kirk, who is the drummer, wears that fuzzy wig, so he holds it on with a sweatband. With the wig and his drumming, he sweats. We all sweat, but he does the most.

"Temple, George and Trip go by impulse. Being lead singer, I have to appear a little unusual. I haven't the elan to carry off anything outrageous. Or the courage to look bizarre. Come give me your opinion." He led her to his dressing room.

There was a leather outfit, which he rejected out of hand. "Too hot. I wore it once in winter at an outdoor concert in TEXAS. The other guys wore coats." He looked at Mab in some indignation. "Who expects it to snow in TEXAS?"

"It snowed!"

"Yeah, but it's not raining inside tonight. What'll I wear?"

There was also a red sequined tank top and red sequined jeans with a blue crotch. He only laughed. "That's been around since David Lee Roth first hit. I haven't the courage to even try it on. If I wore it, I would blush and forget the words. *David* could do it, and it's fun for everyone. I'm not up to his class as an entertainer."

Of the possibles there was a black shirt and trousers. There was a brown outfit, a white one, and one with stripes with a prison motif both up and down or crossways.

"I'm rather conservative," Mab apologized. "I have no idea what to suggest."

"Everyone in the whole outfit, band and Roadies, have their choices. We generally end up drawing straws. It's the one snag in the whole operation—what will Sean Morant wear? What a burden." He carefully put the back of his hand to his forehead in a really lousy mime.

Whoever else had been in the room left then, and they were alone for the first time that day. Tris quickly fastened the door and turned to her. "It's time for my good luck kiss."

While she was deciding if she should, he took her into his arms and pulled her to him slowly. Their eyes were locked, and hers were uncertain. His were yellow fires. He smiled just a little, probably pleased with himself to have her in this position, but she wasn't going to allow anything like this to happen because... because... ummmmm.

It was so nice to be there in his arms. Against him. Harbored there. His arms were so strong around her, holding her. His body such a strong fortress, protecting her.

Fortress? What a word choice. She was a reporter, and words were important to her. She would have to consider that word "fortress" as applied to Tris some... time... later.

He had intended a regular, ordinary kiss. Nice and squishy, but no big deal right now. They were due for makeup pretty soon, and he wasn't going to embarrass her, or himself, by being obvious. But as soon as she came against him, he couldn't resist.

He breathed in harshly as he deepened the kiss and his arms moved to hold her impossibly closer. She wiggled a little to help him do that, and there was a little sound smothered in the back of her throat that set his hair on end.

He groaned with his desire for her, and that shot thrills up her stomach and down into her thighs that made her gasp. She knew she needed to draw back. She knew he wasn't going to let her go until she indicated to him they should not carry on in such a way. In a minute. She couldn't bring herself to stop him yet.

She'd never had a kiss so wildly sensual. She'd never felt such an astonishing reaction to a man's body. Why him? She'd sort that out later. Her hands were in his hair. Her body pressed his, her mouth opened and their tongues met. He trembled, his hands moved and his breath labored.

The door rattled as someone tried to enter. Whoever it was paused, apparently surprised it was barred. There was a thumping knock, and a male voice said, "Makeup in five minutes!"

Only their mouths separated as they stared at each other. That kiss in the hall at the hotel hadn't been a fluke. They had a very serious physical attraction going here. It was frightening to Amabel.

But he seemed ready to explore it further and was seriously frustrated there had been an interruption that couldn't be ignored. "Let's cancel the concert." He actually considered the idea.

She considered agreeing! She gasped at such a reckless rudeness. And she thought immediately that the gasp might not have been at his obvious intentions, but over her own body's reaction to the idea of just running away with him, right then!

Even the skin on her back was excited! Madness! All of it! He still held her. His arms and hands... and his smoldering eyes. His body's heat scorched her, and she could feel his desire.

But modesty, embarrassment and a touch of fright all wound up with her respect for appearances. Her consideration for his state made her pull back, then push her hands on his chest for her release from his reluctant arms. She moved slowly away from him. Their eyes were still caught together.

He stood there, breathing rapidly and high in his chest. His face was very serious. His arms, empty now, slowly dropped to his sides. He tore his eyes from hers and looked at the ceiling.

Then he took a deep breath before he leaned his head down, shaking it sharply to clear it, as he thrust his hands deep into his trouser pockets.

His serious eyes came back to hers, and he smiled at her, his hot eyes then warming in humor. His husky voice blurred a bit, he said, "You must be a witch. You've cast a spell on me. Not that I mind." And he chuckled low in his throat and shook his head again, slowly that time.

Her eyes were like saucers. No other man had ever made her touch the edge of the maelstrom of physical need. The power of it shocked her, that anything could disrupt her control over her body so stunningly.

Don't flirt with danger. That very serious, childhood admonition came to her mind. At that time, not flirting with danger was a warning against talking to friendly strangers, playing with things that blew up, walking on railroad trestles, roller-skating on stairs or crossing streets recklessly.

Later it meant trying drugs, and careless driving; or driving too fast, or allowing a male too many liberties and making his reaction difficult for him, and risky for her.

Now the warning had a whole new interpretation to her. Her body's response to Tris toppled her faith in her stern self-control. And the first questioning of her pride-in-self was to wonder if she was really so pure or if it was only that she'd never been tempted?

She *was* capable of keeping herself from flinging her body back into his arms, but only just. It wasn't a triumph of mind over matter. She still wanted to be there in his arms and feel her body tightly held against his. She would look for the first opportunity. That determination was sobering to her mind, but it made her body twitch in anticipation.

With the next knock on the door, they were both grateful for the first one, for it was his aunt, uncle and a raft of noisy, laughing, affectionate cousins. Their family name was Magee. They were tall, slender people with good clean midwestern faces that would be perfect in a cereal commercial.

"This is Amabel Clayton." Tris put his arm around her. "I do believe the name is already familiar?" There were hoots, and Amabel remembered that his Aunt Trudy wouldn't actually grind her up into the sausage!

Tris then pointed them out. "My Aunt Trudy and my Uncle Finnegan—he's Italian, you can tell—and there's Michael, his wife, Sue, Joe and his wife, Fran, then David and Chuck.

"They're a bunch of freeloaders who clamor for me to come here so they can get free tickets. They keep me broke and, just watch, they'll come along to supper afterwards."

That kind of rough, hair-tousled humor was typical of their relationship. They were cheeky and sassy and loving. They laughed. They raised brief eyebrows over Mab and then accepted her wholeheartedly. It was rather like being set down in a pen with a bunch of romping puppies who refused to be put off.

She took a roll of pictures, and she laughed with the teasing chatter until tears came. The makeup man was patient under the onslaught of assurance that even his skill wouldn't make Sean look human, and they argued loudly over what Sean would wear.

It was Jamie who chose—when had he come in?—and his choice was black cotton silk trousers with a pirate's white, full-sleeved shirt. Mab was surprised; Jamie's taste was perfect.

Tris was patient with them all as they directed what Sean Morant would wear. But his eyes were on Amabel most of the time, simply pleasuring themselves. And she smiled back in a chiding way as she minutely shook her head at him. He'd told her his aunt—and the rest— would have trouble finding subjects to talk about. Yeah. Sure. The noisy mutes did keep the talk and laughter down to a subtle roar.

When it was time to go to their seats, they all kissed Sean's cheeks, but he kissed Mab's mouth, and she was conscious the others exchanged quick smiles with raised, questioning eyebrows. And Jamie watched from under his brows. It made Mab blush.

Their seats were at the rail, up from the floor of the arena. So they were in the front row, above the floor, to the side and even with the stage. They could see. And when the kids all stood up, they could stay seated and still see.

They were in two rows so they could talk and exclaim, among themselves, and they sat Mab in their midst. That could have been like a wildebeest surrounded by a pride of lions, but they simply put her there so that she could hear them all and not feel left out.

On their way inside, the crowd encountered hawkers who sold the band's souvenir headbands, T-shirts, pins and books, all with the group's name and/or pictures. The hawkers had something to fit every budget.

Lighter in their pockets, the audience then poured in through all the entrances and spread like ants at a picnic.

The floor filled with those devotees who would stand for the entire three hours, and the seats were filled with those who would also stand along with all the rest, waving their arms in the air. Seats were redundant.

The warm-up group was a new bunch, and they were good enough so the crowd was kind, but all those there waited for Sean Morant.

Of course, Amabel had watched the videos, and some had been concert-taped, so she knew how the crowds reacted to him. But it was nothing compared to being there and actually witnessing such conduct amid the roar of the crowd.

He came out like a god. He stood as the crowd yelled and yelled, whistling and cheering. As with any skill, the performance was a professional show. The timing was deliberate. Before emotion could peak, there would be comment, or music would begin.

Or in the case of a potential fight, a stern command would be given to behave, or the band would quit playing until they did. The cessation of music made the others in the audience help in keeping the disturbers quiet and orderly.

The rapport between the band and the crowd was interesting. The comments from the stage. The teasing. The use of the town's name. And the laughter of the crowd or cheering.

The music was superb. And Sean Morant was a performer who was skillfully impressive. The songs' words could be understood. The audience sang along. They were touched. The song of comfort for the weary and

hungry of the world had been written after LIVE AID.
It was one of commitment and hope.

There was his song—yelled for—about the way to
treat a woman. And the female part of the audience
laughed and loved it. It made Mab smile—even as she
bristled. She needed to talk to Tris about women. He was
dragging his feet.

There was his song of loneliness, which touched every
heart, telling kids about the need to help themselves. To
crawl out of their shell and help themselves by helping
others. It was a strengthening song for lonely kids who
look with horror on what is being done to our land.

And then Sean said, "This one is new. I've just written it, and it's special to me. I've chosen Fort Wayne for
its tryout. See if you like it." And he sang *The China
Girl.*

Until Tris, as Sean, turned and looked directly at her,
Mab had forgotten Tris knew she was the descendant of
a long-ago China girl. The song was beautiful. And Tris
sang it in his husky voice to her. The seas tossing the
ship, the large, bearded Yankee who stole the girl away
and loved her. It was marvelously done.

Sean looked at the audience, and even turned away
from Mab, as he sang, but he was again looking at
Amabel as he finished, "...and of all the world's
women, he loved the China girl."

The crowd roared its approval and for just a long instant, Tris's eyes stayed on Amabel. On her luminous
blue eyes, on her soft, parted lips. Then reluctantly he
turned away, back to the crowd as he grinned and again
he became Sean Morant.

With the concert's finish, those who had attended
were all depleted—satisfied, exuberantly satisfied—and

they exited the coliseum, leaving the litter of discarded papers, old headbands or T-shirts or bandannas that they had exchanged for their new purchases.

In Sean's dressing room, Mab and his relatives found Sean again in Tris's clothing. His aunt, uncle and cousins chaffed Tris over his performance; he only smiled. Mab interposed tellingly, as she tattled, "They were on their feet and yelling just like everyone else." And she gave them rather cool glances. If she thought to straighten out the Magees and make them tell Tris how good he was, she was mistaken.

His uncle said, "In Italy, they take the opera as seriously as we midwesterners take our Rock. The Italians will give a miserable tenor encore after encore, not in accolade but in trying to get him to do it right!"

They all laughed, even Tris, but Mab chided them. That made Tris's eyes caress her. He wanted to hold her and hear her soft lips say what she thought of his gift of the song. He could hardly wait for his relatives to leave so that he could take Amabel out of there and take her to the motel and make love to her for the rest of the night.

What does a man do when his aunt and uncle take over his life and arrange things to suit themselves? His uncle said, "We're all staying at the big house. There's room for the two of you. We'll take it hard if you should prefer a hotel." And he smiled with the confidence of one who expects not only to have his way, but for the victims to be delighted.

His aunt was equally ignorant of any chance there could be opposition. "And we've food enough to feed an army. You eat out too much, you need a good home-cooked meal."

"Microwaved into submission," Michael put in.

Tris began. "We'll be out for a while tomorrow—"

"I won't hear of it." His Aunt Trudy raised both hands and shook her head as if to discourage a bee. "We'll meet out there, and I'll have everything ready on the table. Sue? Fran? Right?"

They laughed. They were used to Trudy.

With sympathetic grins from his cousins, Tris inquired with some drollness, "We can drive out together? Mab and I?"

Perfectly unsuspecting, Trudy said, "No, if it's more convenient, we could take her along with us, and she wouldn't have to wait around for you."

There comes a time when even a pliant relative must be firm. Tris said in a courteous but no nonsense voice, "She'll go out with me."

"Oh," Trudy said uncertainly. "Well, we'll run along then. Hurry. You do know how to get there?"

"I remember."

"I'm so glad you want to stay with us. This will be such fun."

The cousins all laughed and reached to pat Tris with some sympathy. None of them appeared to notice that no one had ever really asked Mab what she wanted. And her several attempts to explain had been lost in the hubbub.

After Tris's relatives had left, and he was removing his makeup, Mab ventured, "I'll just go on."

But he wasn't as bending with her. He said, "No."

"No one inquired what I wanted."

"Of course not." His reply was very close to being imperial. "They all knew I wanted you with me." And that seemed to be reason enough.

"We need to talk about women's rights."

He paused to look over at her. "You mean it's ka-put? We're back in control? Great! We've been very patient."

"Bite your tongue!"

"Bite *my* tongue?" He was surprised. Then his wicked smile crept out. "There are other things I'd like to do with it."

"I can get a cab."

Deliberately misunderstanding, he objected, "It would cost too much to go clear out to my aunt's in a cab. I'll be through here in just a few minutes."

"There's no reason for me to go out there," she objected.

"For either of us," he agreed. "You know they will put us in separate rooms?"

"I'm not sleeping with you." It cost her a good deal to deny him.

"I know. I know. But our time will come." And he thought he comforted her.

His words jolted her brain, but her body shivered with desire for him. She was being torn apart. While her body and brain argued and debated and quarreled with each other, there was no particularly clear control.

He again looked like Tris. A strange metamorphosis. How amazing. A chameleon.

In something of a stupor, she allowed Tris to put her into her raincoat, take her arm and lead her from the coliseum as he said good-night and thanks to the Roadies they saw along their way outside. Because of Tris's ability to appear ordinary, he was not noted by the people who waited for Sean Morant to leave.

Under a threatening, heavy sky, Tris pitched his things into the car's trunk, and she just stood there. He opened the door and helped her into the car, then closed it and went around to his side. She just sat there, mute.

He settled himself, started the car, leaned across to kiss her very nicely, then he skillfully eased the car into motion, exited the parking lot, turned right onto Parnell and then left on the by-pass and on west of the city. She didn't say anything.

While her mind and body were carrying on their struggle for dominance, which she ignored, there was still some leftover space in her brain that had time for a philosophical musing on what on earth was happening to her orderly life and times?

That rapidly deteriorated into another heated debate. There was the pro and con as in any disagreement. One saying Tris was the most marvelous thing that could happen to any woman, opposed by the snide rejoiner that since she'd known him such a short time, she was certainly a good judge of men.

The pro part said but look how sweetly he'd treated her. And the con part recalled the photographic setup outside the hotel in Los Angeles.

She was rather amazed all the simultaneous debates could go on inside her. She thought how complicated a single unit of humanity could be in order to carry on two quarrels at once inside of itself.

Still another part of her brain viewed her astonishment over this second contention with some irritation. It reminded her that the brain was capable of a great deal more then we've ever suspected, and this was a good indication of a *minimum* of its potential.

It might do well for her to note that while the various quarrels were going on inside her, she was still breath-

ing, swallowing, blinking, and all her other functions—
like her blood being pumped around and cleaned, and
her sitting up straight—were still being cared for. The
admonition sounded suspiciously like that of an unap-
preciated housekeeper.

So although Mab continued being aware of the origi-
nal struggle, the spin-off—concerning her judgment of
men—and the philosophical bemusement, still another
segment considered the marvel of the human brain and
body.

It was no wonder she was somewhat distracted, but
her eyes allowed her brain to register where they were.
And that shortly put a damper on the other parts of her
awareness—although she realized none of the sections
stopped. They did continue to debate.

What roused her to the immediate was the fact Tris
had turned off the highway and parked. They were in a
side lane that appeared to be a farmer's gravel access to
fields, and before he had shut off the engine, Tris had
turned the car to head back toward the highway. It was
after midnight and very quiet. There wasn't a house
anywhere around.

She asked, "What's the matter?"

"I have to kiss you."

With that kind of support, her body took over. She
reached out her hands to grab him, as his closed around
her, and their mouths met eagerly. The sounds of his
breathing quickly became very harsh. He lifted away
from her to open her coat and pushed his hands inside
to slide his arms around her body—clad in her twill
trousers, shirt and sweater vest.

She was limp. Her feeble hands toyed in his hair, her
fingertips touched his face and her head wobbled on her
weak neck. All that while her body was stuck on
wowowowwow sounds. The rest of her mental debaters

teamed up in criticism of her conduct, commenting on her feebleness, her lack of backbone, her victimish appearance, her—cooperation.

But then Tris kissed her again, and sounds faded away except for his disturbed breathing. And her body reveled in the onslaught of sensation, making her gasp and squirm minutely, and a thin little moan escaped to sound in the back of her throat.

That caused a ragged groan from him, and he hugged her to him so tightly, his hands were so hard and his fingers dug so, in trying to get her closer, that she would probably have bruises in a day or two.

He finally lifted his face from hers and his voice was gravelly. "Did you like my song for you?"

"Oh, yes." She managed to form the words quite well.

That instigated another passionately stormy embrace, before he raised his head to say, "We have to go. They'll be waiting."

She lay in his arms and swallowed slowly and rather loudly. It was with some difficulty, as if something wasn't working quite right—or perhaps was distracted? Her whole mind was in a swoon. Her body a languid welcome. Her skin erotically filmed with sweat from wearing a coat on such a still, ominous, humid night.

He ran a trembling hand over her very clothed stomach, and she moved in pleasure. Then that hand went slowly to her sensitive rib cage and spread there, just under her breast, as he kissed her another of his stunning, mind-bending kisses.

When had he learned to kiss such a way? Who had taught him? Well . . . he *was* thirty-six.

Her eyes opened, for a segment of her brain was chattering along as to why her rib cage would be so sensitive to his hand. Was it because—as a woman—she had been constructed partly from a man's rib? And his touching it reminded her of how much she was a part of him?

Tris changed the kiss, his tongue caressing, and she forgot ribs. He barely lifted his mouth and his lips touched and pulled at hers as he whispered, "We have to go."

She wasn't a whole lot of help.

As he lifted his head so that he could see her eyes in the strange night's light, his hand curled up over her breast to hold, to squeeze and massage.

Her lips parted and her shoulders moved so that he had to kiss her again. He moved his head to the side of hers and held her tightly. "I haven't been in this kind of bind in years! What are you doing to me?" His whisper was ragged and his hands feverish.

His kiss then was so intense and held such hunger that her emotions spilled into tears. All the longing in her own body, all the frustration, all the mental debate—she was so pulled and torn that she wept.

He held her tenderly, and in that husky, passion-roughened voice he told her, "Shhh. It's going to be all right. You can't help being the most fortunate woman God ever made. I forgive you for driving me mad. Oh, Amabel, my Mab."

And he gave her tiny, sweet kisses along her wet cheek, and he stroked back her hair, making a mess of it. "I wish we could have had tonight alone." He was so regretful. "But we do have to get to my aunt's. Mab, we have to go."

It was as if she was being difficult about leaving!

He sighed in a shaky breath. "Are you okay now?"

She nodded.

He kissed her gently. Released her with great reluctance. Then he started the car, eased it into motion and drove as he took quick looks at her. "Do you have a comb?"

She got her purse and began repairs.

Skillfully, quickly, he drove to make up time. How silly. When they finally got there, everyone was almost dull, they had waited so long. His aunt gave him an inadvertent out. "It was the turn at Johnson's, right?"

Tris grinned. "Right. I sailed on through it as if I was driving a hot knife through butter."

His cousins laughed immoderately.

Tris was a little pale. He ate reasonably. Mab pushed at the food on her plate. The chatter went on around her. They were nice people. They were glad to see Tris, and their affection was apparent.

It wasn't until they were almost finished with the late meal that his Aunt Trudy really looked at Amabel. "Why, you're exhausted!" She was appalled. Her spare, golf-playing body hid a maternal heart.

Aunt Trudy rose and took Amabel's arm. "You poor child! I shall get you to bed immediately. Up you go. Chuck! Get her things, please, dear. Bring them up to the middle room by the stairs."

Tris's cousins all laughed in delighted sympathy.

Tris half rose, "I'll—"

"Sit still," his aunt commanded. "We know how long it takes you to wind down after a concert. We all napped today so we can keep you company."

Seven

Led by Tris's Aunt Trudy, Mab went up the stairs, not really listening to his aunt's kind chatter. With routine dispatch, Mab was bustled into the hall bath, the shower was turned on and towels were laid out. She was admonished to just rinse off in the hot water in order to relax.

As Mab turned off the spray and opened the broadcloth curtain, she saw a gown had been hung on the doorknob. It was easier to simply put it on rather than to mention she had a gown in her case. It was the course of least resistance.

She emerged from the bathroom to find Aunt Trudy was opening windows down from the top and up from the bottom as, oddly, she said something about *winds* in that still, humid night.

Trudy told Mab, "If it should get bad, we'll go down to the fruit cellar in the basement. That's just down the stairs, to the left, through that door and on down into the basement. You don't have to remember, we'll not forget you're here."

Aunt Trudy followed Amabel into the bedroom as she continued. "Now hop into bed and sleep. Don't worry about a thing. I'll prop the door open, so it won't slam shut with the wind. If you know anything about them, you know air pressure is the problem.

"Don't worry if it should rain in. A little rain won't hurt anything too much. We need to equalize the air pressure, if it comes. Now sleep tight. Don't worry."

And Tris's aunt bent over and kissed Amabel's forehead—in her hurried, efficient way—before she bustled out, leaving Amabel alone in the big, too big bed.

Whatever Mab wasn't supposed to worry about, she wouldn't. Aunt Trudy was perfectly capable of handling anything at all. Mab had enough to worry about all by herself. And she had the time for it.

She had had a nap on the chairs at the coliseum. She wasn't physically tired. She was only worn-out with frustrated desire and mental debate.

Apparently, Tris had assumed her tears were from frustration alone. Did that mean he was foiled only by lack of opportunity? He had no debate? His mind was placidly, simply waiting for events? He assumed the reality of her seduction.

Was she the only one who wondered about this mindless attraction—such hungry need on such short acquaintance? Instead of taking time for a long, drawn-out courtship and reasonable care in his selection, was he used to simply hopping into bed and getting it over?

Then Mab was the only one who had qualms. Only she was troubled by whether or not this overwhelming need should be indulged? Was that all she felt for Tris?

Or all he wanted of her? She wasn't a man hater. She simply wasn't a bed hopper.

But she wanted Tris.

Of all the men she'd met, why him? That halves of oranges explanation didn't hold water. There would be a thousand men in this world who would be exactly as attractive, as clever, as charismatic, as desirable and as beautifully made. They could even have eyes as heart-stopping with their yellow golden fires. There could be another whose mouth was as demanding, as tender. Another whose hands . . .

Well, there were other men who would be as attractive as Tristan Roald. Another as talented. As . . . There *was* no other man! Not to her knowledge. And in her lifetime, she might never find another like him! This night was probably the only time she would have a chance to be with him! Tomorrow they would part and she would go on to L.A. alone. Alone.

She lay there trying to plot a way to separate him from his relatives. She could go downstairs in Aunt Trudy's nice, cotton nightgown and say, "Would you excuse Tris? I need a word with him."

Then what would she say—to him?

She could say, "I believe you wouldn't be unwilling. Would you mind coming up to bed with me?"

He would shriek and clutch his clothes to him. No, he wouldn't.

He's say, "I'd love to, but they're waiting for me to visit with them. Sorry." He'd be polite about it. It was something all those other women would do, those who'd shared photos with him.

Or she could wait until the family was all in bed, then she could search him out. How? Go around knocking on doors and inquiring who was inside until she finally found his room? That would be blatant and quite embarrassingly clumsy.

She restlessly turned over in bed. She wasn't cut out for this. No one had ever told her how to go about this kind of thing. How maddening. Seducing a man had never entered her mind before Tris. Other women did it. What were the signals? Other women did have affairs. How did they instigate them?

Faintly she could hear the laughter downstairs. And she eventually heard the soft steps and careful whispers as some of the others came to bed. She heard the outside door open, at the back of the house, and men's voices floated up for her to hear their soft male laughter. Then she heard faint sounds of a basketball hitting a backboard and bouncing on hard-packed ground.

Tris and his cousins were playing basketball at that time of night. There were five of them in that span of age—between the last of the twenties and into the thirties. They were tiring Tris so he could sleep. The winddown from the pitch of the concert. And—unknowingly—from sexual frustration. And what was she to do?

She could go down, in that white cotton nightgown, and make their number six, and they could then play shirt and skin. She could be on the shirt side. Sure.

They would *know* what a fix she was in. They'd understand exactly why she was down there shooting baskets at that time of night. They'd snigger and . . . they'd all know. They sure would.

She shifted her hungry body's position in that big bed, and she sighed in boredom.

She wakened later. Roused to realize Aunt Trudy's predicted winds had come. They were erratic and gusty.

There were spats of rain and it was cooler. Mab pulled up another quilt and snuggled down again to sleep.

Still later, she sat up in bed, wide-eyed and scared. The winds were roaring, the rains poured down, and the lightning cracked shockingly bright as the thunder made the bed tremble and its springs hum.

There were shouts, and Tris was there, dressed. "Hurry! Just grab your clothes. Come on."

He took her blanket from the bed, and she managed to snatch her sweater vest and trousers. He took her sneakers. The family was pouring down the stairs in a noisy stream. "Everybody here? Chuck?"

"Yo."

"The girls?" Uncle Finnegan questioned. "Give me your hand, Trudy."

"We've got the girls."

"Amabel?" Aunt Trudy questioned.

"She's with me," Tris replied.

When they reached the first floor, the winds were tearing at the trees. The house shook and shuddered. It was very intimidating. People feel they control their lives, and then nature does something rash to prove what's in charge and how ineffectual they actually are.

"What is it?" Mab's voice was almost lost in the storm's fury.

Down into the basement they poured. Talking, exclaiming, excited. That's what surprised Amabel; they were all excited. No fear. Just stimulation!

The fruit cellar was dug back into the ground from the basement. There were two entrances. One from the outside, set into a mound, and one from the basement. That gave Amabel pause to consider: This was a dangerous situation! If that adventuresome family was taking precautions, something serious was going on.

Someone turned on a battery lamp, and they un-
stacked some simple benches. "It won't last long," Uncle Finnegan comforted them. "Turn on the radio, one
of you."

The sound of the report had picked up in tempo from
the usual weatherman drone. And Whitney County was
being warned, "Take cover."

They had. They were insulated there. Sounds filtered
in, when they were quiet. The storm raged on around
them. Something crashed. They exchanged looks with
raised eyebrows.

Finnegan groaned, "The stock."

"The dog," David anguished. "I whistled for him,
but even he was probably smart enough to already take
cover."

The weatherman went on with specific reports.
Warning them there were a series of tornadoes. Not to
leave shelter too soon.

Bug-eyed, Mab whispered, "A tornado?"

Tris had her wrapped in the blanket and in his arms.
"Apparently more than one. You're safe here."

It is telling to see how people respond to unusual circumstances. In that brief time, Mab was convinced that
if it ever came to a holocaust, she wanted to be with
them, and specifically with Tris. Her fortress. She was
surrounded by him. There were smiles from the others,
in that battery light, but Tris didn't adjust his embrace
to a less protective one. Or a less selfish one. He held her.

It was she who slowly extricated herself from his reluctant arms. She didn't want to leave his shelter, but she
disliked appearing such a wimp before those casual
people. She was just as brave as they.

But her sneaky body mourned their presence. If she
and Tris were there alone, she could allow him to com-

fort her...to the sound of all that fury venting itself out there. And safe and snug, they would make love. Wildly, like the storm.

She looked at the others, wondering if they could ever guess what she was thinking, and she saw Sue touch her husband, Michael, and smile at him. Sue, too. And probably Fran over there by Joe? Joe put his hand on Fran's nape and barely shook her.

Mab lied into the silence, "We don't have tornadoes out where I live in a more civilized, more welcoming land."

Uncle Finnegan exclaimed, "How fortunate you were to come to Indiana in time to witness this one!"

Mab grinned, and a little competitiveness stirred. "Well, we do have the Pacific, which can be impressive in a storm, but it stays pretty much contained. It doesn't swamp the land entirely."

Uncle Finnegan nodded and commented, "Pacific means peaceful." He'd dismissed the entire Pacific as not much of a threat.

So Amabel was forced to mention, "But we have brushfires that are a nuisance, especially if one's house is in the path—and we have rain on occasion, then mud slides, but no tornadoes."

Tris's crinkles deepened as he reminded her, "And there are the earthquakes."

"They do tend to disorient one." She did admit that.

As they all laughed, Tris said something about his song.

She realized he said something, but it was lost as she was saying rather airily, "We are supposed to break off from the continent and slide into the Pacific."

There were agreements and comments, but Tris shook his head. "No, when a big one comes, it will raise up a whole new mountain range, and Los Angeles will become an inland, landlocked city, lost in the new desert between ranges."

Rather stubbornly she persisted. "We'll break off and slide into the sea."

"If you will notice." He was courteous. "Horrendous earthquakes have happened before. A series of them. From the Rockies west to the Sierra Nevadas, then the Sierra Madres, to the San Gabriels just east of Los Angeles."

"The experts say we'll break off." There was a streak of stubborn in any of Ezekiel's descendants.

Tris dismissed experts. "What do they know?"

All in all, that noisy bunch sided with Tris. When Mab didn't agree, it was Finnegan who coaxed, "Wouldn't it be better for the city to be saved than to have it drowned?"

She explained, "I always thought our city would become another Atlantis, and Jacques Cousteau would be there to perfect his valve implant that would allow us to breathe either air or the seawater, whichever way we wanted it."

"Cousteau?" someone questioned.

"His anniversary was just for his *first* seventy-five years. He's in good, sleek shape. He'll last two more sessions of seventy-five years. That'll be two hundred twenty-five all told and that should be enough for him this time."

Trudy said, "What an inventive man! If there's a way for a valve to be invented to breathe either air or water, he would figure it out. He was the one who invented the aqualung."

They talked of fishing, swimming, lakes, rivers and rafting. They all entered into the discussion, until the weather station said the tornado warning had been downgraded to a watch. That meant while the weather had potentially tornado producing conditions, no new funnels had been sighted.

The station continued, saying there were reports of severe damage and asking those listening to check on their neighbors. Lines were down, making communications difficult. And they gave the emergency citizens band channel to use for desperate need.

The listeners were told which channels had been set aside for information from emergency stations now being manned by ham radio volunteers in the courthouses of each county.

As the weather report repeated, Amabel said, "I'm impressed."

"We are prepared," Finnegan agreed. "We've never really needed it. We organized in my dad's time, during World War II. It continued with the Cold War, and then with the weather. We've never needed it too badly."

But it was needed then.

They had a tough time getting free of the fruit cellar. A tree had fallen against the house; the naked, shattered roots outside had jammed that door and the shifting of the house frame jammed the inside door. Being prepared, they had an ax. They hit the door a couple of telling blows, then used one of the benches as a battering ram to force their way out.

Had they been in the actual path of the tornado, the house would have been gone. It wasn't. There was damage from the peripheral winds, which was more than enough, but all could be repaired.

They all went outside in that stormy predawn to look, and the blustery winds were strong, petulant and difficult. The clouds roiled and threatened. Mab held Tris's big, warm hand.

The large, shaggy, mixed-breed dog came directly to Tris. Mab watched as its nose nudged Tris's hand from his pocket with a practiced movement and got its head under Tris's hand before the hand could be moved. And Tris petted the dog.

How smart of the dog to come to Tris. Her fortress. Fortress? How strange for an independent woman to need a man as her protection! She'd think about the foolishness of such a thought—another time.

She leaned against Tris and lay her head on his chest. His arm tightened as he looked down at her and smiled.

The stock was very alert but apparently not too disturbed. The barn had survived. The chickens were restless, and the horses came to the fence and whickered. All the animals looked in the southwest direction, from which tornadoes tended to form. Did they know that?

They're called dumb animals. But Amabel had watched animals do marvelous things. And look how the dog had manipulated Tris into comforting it.

They were all together again—and the dog was leaning against Tris's leg, his head under Tris's hand. The dog's eyes were closed in peace. Mab mentioned how clever the dog had been to come to Tris for comfort.

Chuck laughed. "That dog? He's so dumb he probably didn't notice there *was* a storm! And he does that all the time. He just looks for someone idle, and he gets himself petted. You could make a career out of petting that dog."

Like her. But she just wanted to be petted by Tris.

Most of the men left, after grabbing some of Trudy's rolls from the freezer and pouring coffee into thermoses.

They'd reported in on the special CB channel and offered their four-wheelers. They were asked to check their neighbors and then gather in Columbia City.

If they weren't needed there, they could go back home. But to come in for now until they knew the extent of the damage. It looked bad. Really bad.

The news came in gradually. A staggering number of electrical and phone lines around Fort Wayne were down. All the backups had been blown away. With spotty exceptions, there was no electricity in all of northeastern Indiana. The freaky storms had wreaked such damage!

The weather bureau was tabulating and verifying the tornadoes that had touched down, and it was incredible. There had been almost a dozen. That was the first count.

There simply weren't enough trucks to go around to all those willing to help. So Tris and his cousin Chuck were kept at home to make emergency repairs on the barn.

Trudy put a great pot on the bottled gas stove and began a soup. She had no idea how many she might be feeding or housing, but she would be ready. If no one needed it, she would freeze what they didn't eat.

The first bunch who came were neighbor children. The neighbor's house had been demolished! Safely in their storm cellar, no humans were hurt. They'd lost a cow and some chickens. They couldn't find their cat.

The parents were seeing what could be salvaged from the wreckage. The children were small, too young to risk in the wreckage, so they were at the Magees'.

Trudy put them to work. That was the best way to be distracted. And it was Tris who organized and supervised them! Even eight-year-olds knew who Sean Morant was.

He had them moving half-grown chicks to a repaired shed. While doing that, he taught the children how much wood a woodchuck chucked when a woodchuck could chuck wood.

Tris helped Chuck, who was labeled a woodchuck with great hilarity, and he sighed patiently over it. From there, they went to rubber baby buggy bumpers and the kids laughed until they had to sit down.

After that, the overstimulated kids went inside to help there. Calming them, Aunt Trudy contrived chores for the children. Then she settled them down to making cloverleaf rolls. They rolled the dough in small rounds, easy for small hands, and it was a soothing time.

Then the two men left at the farm replaced long boards on one side of the barn that the wind had torn loose. With the lessening winds, they got up on that high roof and patched it in order to protect the rest of the bales of hay stored inside the barn.

They were ignoring the house and that fallen tree for the moment. They would find time to fix it later. Now, only vital things were being done.

Amabel, and Trudy's daughters-in-law, Sue and Fran, were chopping onions and various colored cabbages for the soup. The meat had been thawed in the boiling water and soon the aroma from the simmering pot filled the house. Great bags of frozen vegetables, from last summer's garden, would be added to the pot, and Aunt Trudy then turned her attention to the rolls being formed.

Pots of coffee were made and kept hot. Men stopped by and refilled their thermoses. They sat at the kitchen table as they ate pancakes, ham and eggs. Those men brought the rest of them up to current on what was going on, and what had happened to who.

It was an interesting experience for a reporter. Mab took notes, and took wonderful pictures of the tired, hungry men. She asked, "May I go with you? Or could I borrow a Jeep?"

They replied, "Not this time. Not yet. And we can't spare a car or truck yet. If we should find someone hurt, and have to take them in, to the hospital, you would have to stay behind somewhere and it might not be safe."

"I've had first aid. I've had disaster training. I could help."

"There are reports of looters. We found a man who had been blown into a tree and badly hurt. He wondered if anyone would ever come to help him. His leg was broken, he faded in and out of consciousness. And a car came along.

"He saw a man get out and began to climb up to him, and he was thanking God for hearing his prayers when the man took his wallet from his back pocket, took the money from it, dropped the wallet to the ground, climbed down from the tree, picked up the TV from the roofless living room and *left!*"

"Incredible!"

"We wouldn't have believed it, either, but we were the ones that took him out of the tree, there was his wallet on the ground, the tire tracks of the truck and the TV table empty. We called in to report it when we took the guy in to the hospital.

"There's been a couple of incidents. A woman was standing in the middle of what was left of her house, looking around, when a car drove up. She didn't recognize them, but she thought they'd come to help. And she watched as a man and woman came over, and pawed through her things, then walked off with her television and a wooden chair! Never said a word, any of them.''

"How can people behave in such a way?'' Mab, the seasoned reporter, was appalled.

"Those are boggling the few it's happened to. But then we see all those around who are the people who've helped. God, what would we do without people who help out?''

And through that whole time, they heard about the helpers. Men who came in pickups with tools to concoct shelter. People who chased down livestock, rounded them up and fixed fences. People who helped people, and Tris Roald was one.

There were far more of the helpers than ever there were looters. People can be so offhandedly helpful, so impulsively generous. And they worked as hard as those whose property it was.

Tris was finally given an area map and a four-wheel-drive Jeep of a man who had to sleep. Tris reported in at Columbia City to see the map and where to go to help those who needed help.

Only Chuck was home then to do his mother's bidding and to help his sisters-in-law in trying to keep her from overdoing.

The human traffic through the Magee house was staggering. Then one trip, Tris was alone, and Mab got to go as partner for him. Since she was with the Los Angeles based *Adam's Roots*, she was qualified to see how Indiana natives managed.

At the emergency headquarters, they had blankets put in the Jeep, the marked map, beef broth, sandwiches, water and a first-aid kit. Being in their situation, one never knows what they'll need. They went out that afternoon, following their directions.

There was the rumor of a new family who had just parked a house trailer somewhere off the track. The helicopters weren't available yet for an air search. However, as the choppers took the worst cases into Fort Wayne, or down to Indianapolis, and returned, they were also watching for distress signals.

Tris's map was marked with those who had been contacted and were okay. Circled in red were those who might know about the rumored missing people. They stopped and questioned those people as they went along.

"Yeah," said one. "I heard something about that, too. New family. Bought some land west of here, or southwest. Ask at the Lowells. They might know. Here, let me see your map, I can show you."

But the Lowells said, "No. Not that we heard about. But we just got back from TEXAS. We're Winter TEXANS, you know. Too bad the phone lines are down. And the CB's swamped with chatter. But you might go by the Magees. They know everybody."

"They're my relatives," Tris explained. "We're staying with them. They've only heard the rumor. We would just like to be sure, if there are some strangers, that they're all right."

"Well, you could go to the general store, it's just a little place but—let me show you on the map. If there's any new people out this way, they'd of heard, at the store."

They found tree-blocked roads and blessed the Jeep's ruggedness. They were shocked by the storms' devastation. Big trees, standing stripped and stump-armed, were mute testimony to the fury of the storms.

They found a dog alone, but he wouldn't allow them to approach. They marked his location, for he guarded a destroyed house. They left food nearby and hand-pumped well water into a bucket for him.

The searchers found people who'd heard someone might have moved onto some land but could give no real direction. They stopped for gas twice. And as they drove along, they talked as they searched through the countryside that late afternoon. They reported in to emergency headquarters. And they stopped and ate on a lane out in the middle of nowhere.

The concert had been less than twenty-four hours before. They'd had very little sleep. And they were both very tired. The wind was still strong; the clouds whipped along and the air was chilly.

Tris called in on the CB to ask, "About those new people in a house trailer, have you heard anything more concrete? We've been chasing our tails."

"The mother of the wife called for information. But their mailing address is General Delivery, here in Columbia City. We have their names—Ken and Tracy Harris. There's a kid. A little girl. Katy. Someone is going to look up deeds and land titles tomorrow to get us a better location. Let it go for tonight."

"We'll look off the road as far as we can until it's too dark."

"Appreciate it."

After that they drove wearily in silence for a while until Mab said, "If they are hurt..."

And Tris said, "Yeah."

It was just after five o'clock when they stopped on a hill and got out field glasses for another look around. It was a wooded area, so observation was restricted, but the light was going and there was just the chance...

They moved stiffly. With the wind still strong, the sky was beginning to clear. It would be a beautiful day tomorrow. They searched carefully with the field glasses and saw nothing. They looked at each other and again carefully searched as far as they could see.

There wasn't even a road in sight to indicate there was any civilization at all. They could have been alone out there. The meadows were small; there was the glint of a lake about two city blocks away surrounded by evergreens and a forest of tree skeletons. One of the tornado paths of destruction had quite obviously plowed through the lonely land.

Soon it would be spring. All this would become a paradise. The leaves would burst forth, the fields would be plowed, stock would be turned out to graze, and all the land would be renewed.

Tris went to the Jeep and put the field glasses tiredly into their case. He turned and leaned against the side of the vehicle and looked at Mab.

She smiled slightly, equally tired, and went to him. "We'd better go back. Off the road like this, we could get lost in the dark."

"We have blankets, food and water. I'll call in saying we can't make it back, and we'll stay here tonight." His eyes were glowing coals ready to ignite.

"Why, Mr. Roald, you Viking!"

He frowned at her in some exaggeration. "I'll probably sleep. I'm beat down to my nub."

"Thank goodness." She gasped with some drama. "I'll be safe."

He tilted his head back and looked at her over his cheekbones as he pushed up his lower lip. He commented in a slow drawn-out manner, "Maybe not entirely."

Eight

On the hood of the Jeep, Mab poured them each a cup of broth. She set out the individually wrapped sandwiches of egg or ham salad. And she faced the fact that she was going to be spending the night out there, in the wilds of Indiana, with Tristan Roald. The Viking.

She smiled.

This wasn't exactly the way she had intended to make love with him, out of the middle of nowhere, on the ground. She'd be on the bottom with her back to the hard ground, and he'd be on top.

How like a man to assume that position. Knowledgeable men had to've invented sexual coupling, in that manner, to be on top.

She'd thought if it did happen, it would be in a bed. Perhaps one with satin sheets on which to slip and slide a little. She'd be wearing something sexy.

And it would have been a full, classic seduction with yearnings and touches and kisses that thrilled their souls.

She looked over at Tris. He was really tired. She looked around. There wouldn't even be a darkened room.

Instead they would have a night-darkened sky for their ceiling, in their horizon-to-horizon room. There would be no candlelight, wine or flowers. No soft music. From what she'd heard, those were the ingredients for the usual seduction.

Instead they could have the flashlight on. She had a Walkman in her bag that would provide a little sound. And the beef broth would be elixir. Actually, with Tris, rainwater in a mud hole would be elixir.

He came up behind her and slid his strong hands around her intensely self-conscious body. He held her close to him, tightly back against the length of his hard body. He nuzzled his evening whiskers between her shoulder and the side of her face. That gave her goose bumps in intimate places and her breasts got pushy. He kissed her cheek very sweetly and moved his hands up to her breasts.

It was going to happen, there, in that tattered, storm-wrecked place.

Her throat was foggy and the words blurred. "I hesitate to ask if you'd like some broth and sandwiches?"

His rusty voice was smoky with desire. "I want you."

"I suspected."

He turned her in his hands so that she faced him. He asked as if indignant, "Did you suspect? What tipped you off? I thought I was very subtle."

"It would be interesting to see you blatant if that was an example of subtle."

"I can be blatant."

"Yes."

Being blatant, he asked, "Do you need the dark to undress?" His eyelashes dropped over his eyes as he looked down her body.

She gasped, "You want me to take off my clothes, out here, in this windy, wide-open country, on top of a hill?" She looked around, feeling exposed.

He shrugged even as he held her. "No one else is here."

"You are." She tilted her head as she looked up at him.

His reply was instant and therefore seemingly open and uncalculated. "I'm the other half of you." He was solemn. More gently, he placated her. "You don't have to be embarrassed with me."

She went back a notch to inquire, "Half of me? Somehow it's just a bit difficult for me to see you as any part of being female."

He admitted, "I am a male." And he looked at her with amused laughter in his brown-golden eyes.

She considered his words before she agreed, "I'll vouch for it."

"And male and female are complementary," he lectured to expand her knowledge. "Therefore one of each makes a pair. Halves."

"I see. Clever."

He put a forefinger beneath her chin and gently raised her face to his and his husky voice asked softly, "Are you delaying because you're shy? Or are you reluctant to be close to me?"

Her blue, blue eyes lifted to his, and she smiled very faintly. "Surely not."

"Come see your bed." He took her hand and turned away.

"It's early yet." While her arm extended as her hand was carried the two steps with him, it slid out of his light grasp and returned to curl on her chest. Otherwise, she didn't move.

He looked back at her. "Don't pretend not to want me." He held out his hand to her.

"I...really do." She licked her lips and her eyes flicked around before she bit into her lower lip. She looked right at him then, and her eyes turned his heart over in his chest as she put her hand in his.

"Me, too."

She admitted with some shyness, "I've never been a part of such a rampant desire."

"As bad as rampant?" He smiled and her hand in his felt cool to his heat.

She nodded in tiny head bobs that appeared a bit nervous. "Devastating."

He had led her the few steps to the ground sheet with its covering of blankets. "You might have just casually mentioned that you wanted me that badly."

She was honest. "I thought I was more than obvious."

He considered. Then he chided with some inner amusement, "You hid it quite well."

"I was all over you!" she protested in indignation. "I've been carrying on like a madwoman! Didn't you even notice?"

He narrowed his eyes as he searched his memory. "I do recall a twitch or two."

"And the moaning and groaning!" she exclaimed. "I was so embarrassed."

He laughed so low and sexy, and the flames leaped in his brown eyes. "Is that why you blushed?"

"Yes." She readily admitted it. "I thought I would shock you."

"No one's around," he said as he looked around. "Why don't you try shocking me now?"

"It's still daylight!" she protested in really fake indignation. "And we're out here in the open with no doors or window shades—"

His hoarse voice coaxed, "Let me see you."

She twitched a controlled restlessness. "I'm a little awkward about this." She didn't think her saying it surprised him.

Reasonably he inquired, "Why?"

She shrugged and looked at him very seriously. "I'm not into bed hopping."

"Only one bed," he soothed. "And it's just blankets on the bare ground."

How strange to understand herself. She admitted to him, "It seems a little scandalous."

"I've never known you to be so chatty." He teased her gently. "*Are* you delaying? It's your fate. Come along with me and be my love."

She looked around the torn Eden. And she was delaying. "You're sure you wouldn't rather eat first while it's light enough to see?"

"Quite sure." He gathered her against his chest.

His arms were encircling her and his eyelashes were longer than she'd thought. "Tris..."

But he kissed her then. He bent her back over his arm and did it perfectly. He did the kiss quite beautifully, too.

When he lifted his head, she lay there in his arms and smiled at his smile as she complimented him. "You're quite good at this sort of thing. What's next? I'm not sure how to act."

"I know exactly what to do. There's a little book in the first-aid kit that—"

"How?" she interrupted.

"I read very quickly while you were putting out the food. It says if the opportunity arises . . . bend her back over your arm and kiss her. She'll swoon. Are you swooning?" He frowned at her and considered her. "You aren't even affected!"

She closed her eyes, put the back of one hand to her forehead and heaved a great, swooning sigh.

He became efficient as he moved and took her by her arms. "Then it says you put her down on the ground, and get to it."

She frowned and opened her eyes. "That seems a little abrupt. You must have skipped a step or two."

He shrugged as he explained the obvious. "Well, in a first-aid kit instruction booklet, which explains sunstroke, snakebites and broken bones, there isn't a whole lot of room to go into too much detail on side issues. I suppose if I was going to do it right, I should go to a library and research it properly." He nodded as if that was probably what he should do.

"Properly?" she questioned the use of that particular word. "I would think a seduction of a maiden lady could not, in all good grace, be called . . . proper." She subtly licked her bottom lip in concentration as she considered the problem.

"That hadn't occurred to me." He appeared surprised. It was well-done. He inquired, "Do you mean I'm supposed to do this *im*properly? That's a disturbing thought."

Being helpful, she suggested, "You could kiss me again."

"No." He shook his head. "I did the last one, this time it's your turn. Equal rights extends to men, too. Right? Then I deserve equal time and consideration and attack."

She thought about it before she commented, "You weren't attacking me."

"Not...quite...yet." His smile was absolutely wicked.

So, blushing, she wound her arms around his head and kissed him very nicely.

He made a long *mmm* sound of appreciation that caused the most curious little squiggle to begin in the core of her.

Then it was his turn, and he did a magnificent job of that kiss. Then hers again, and by then they were down on the ground, on that rough blanket bed of seduction, in the fading but still quite strong daylight.

He told her gently, "If I pull up this blanket, you won't freeze while I remove your jacket."

A little breathless, she didn't object.

He tossed her jacket over onto the Jeep as he suggested, "You could help me take off mine."

Reclining as she was, half under him, she did that awkwardly. He had to do most of it. He was just so big, leaning over her, for her to reach around. But she did struggle earnestly and quite seriously to do her part.

He watched her and laughed. "You are a treat."

She considered the word. "Ice-cream cone and lollipop type treat?"

He was sure. "Naw. Sexy, seduction treat."

"Ahhh." She acknowledged the caution. "You seem quite sure I'm going through with this."

"Umm-hmmm."

"Well—I—am!" Her admission was interesting because it was assumed that until then she had thought she could have stopped at any time. But with her words, she had crossed the deciding line. It surprised her even then that she really, fully intended to make love with him. How rash of them both! "Is there any poison ivy?"

"I looked." He chuckled again. Deliciously low and amused. He peeled off her sweater and blouse. She tugged for cover, but he held it up and looked at her. "Beautiful. Beautiful."

Then he leaned down to her and kissed her thoroughly. His hands caressed her body. Then he moved his whiskers over her face quite gently. Then a little rougher into her neck and on down her chest as he carefully mouthed, then rubbed his face over her tender breasts.

The contrast—of his hot, wet tongue and those rough whiskers on her cool flesh—caused amazing reactions to riot inside her body. She squeaked, her knees rose and she clutched at his head, holding him hard against her.

Without hurting her, he had a little trouble lifting his head free as he asked, "Help me with my shirt. I want you to touch me."

She was willing. Anything to help their progress. But her fingers fumbled, and he had to take over just to get it done. Her hands moved over his chest, feeling the wiry, hairy mat and the sensation curled her toes inside her sneakers.

His hand smoothed her susceptible, very clothed stomach, as he kissed her again—although it was her turn—then he hovered over her to deliberately rub that crinkly chest pelt over her soft nipples.

He drove her wild. Her back arched her chest up and her knees rubbed together, as she gasped and clutched at him, causing his body to tense and his breathing to become ragged.

Her knees moved so restlessly they called to Mab's mind Wanda Moore. She asked in a whisper, "Did you really make love with Wanda Moore?"

"No," he replied readily enough, but then he questioned from curiosity, "What brought that up?"

"When she said you were 'delicious' she rubbed her knees together. And my knees are rubbing together." She gasped that out.

"Let me feel." He put his big hand down between her trousered knees, but she only clamped her knees tightly together, holding his hand right there. She said urgently, "Tris, please."

"Please ... what?" She couldn't possibly be asking that they stop? He tried to steady himself, to calm down a little.

"Make love to me."

The waves of desire that her words caused to wash over his body and concentrate wickedly, deliciously, made him put his head down by hers. She was such a strange and different woman, she'd had him uncertain. But she really wanted him!

He finally took off her shoes but left her socks on, then he opened her trousers and peeled them off her with hands that trembled. He wanted to look at her lying there, but she was wild.

She attacked his belt and almost sent him over the edge! He had to sit up to untie and get rid of his own shoes, but she was fumbling so badly that he had to undo his trousers. As he was trying to get rid of them down his legs, she clutched at him.

"Hurry," she whispered as her breath panted, and her groping hands were feverish as she strained at his wide shoulders.

He'd really intended to go slowly, to savor this longer, but she was so wild! He leaned over to kiss her, and she pulled him down to her.

By then, his breathing was furnace blasts, and his hot hands scorched her skin as he kneaded her body. His rough palms rubbed her cool satin skin; his fingers spread to take her breast into his hand, to hold it and savor the feel of her.

She was writhing and moaning so that he could no longer resist her. He lay on her to enter her hot, eager body... to stop in shock, then to remove himself from her, falling to one side, to roll over onto his back and lay a forearm across his eyes.

"What's wrong?" She half rose and questioned in the beginnings of alarm. "Are you having a heart attack?"

He gasped the words hopelessly. "You're a virgin!"

"So?" She was indignant and rose to sit naked in the cold air.

"A twenty-eight-year-old virgin! You're probably not even on the Pill."

"What's that got to do with anything?" she demanded with a jerky, hostile breath.

He enunciated carefully, "If you had thought to mention that you were a virgin, I could have gotten you some protection!"

"If I'm not worried about it," she asked indignantly, "why should you?"

He sighed with an exasperated huff and was silent. Then thoughtfully he said, "Actually you've been sending me clear signals all along, if I'd been paying closer attention. I've never known a more modest, more hyper woman."

Her eyes were almost feverish. Her voice stumbled. "Aren't you—are you... quitting?"

"I have no protection for you." He removed his arm and gave her a reasonable stare.

"And you call yourself a Viking!" She was just a bit scornful. But mostly frustrated. Actually, she was goading him.

"The protection is vital." He was excessively patient as he explained, "I couldn't make love with you, Amabel, and not go to completion. I want you very, very much." Then, deliberately speaking the words to emphasize them, he said, "I am doing a very remarkable job of sternly controlling myself. You really ought to be impressed."

"Balderdash!" She totally dismissed being impressed by his control. "And you claimed your middle name was Ezekiel! Bah!"

He moved. He rolled up with an effortless coil of muscles he told her, "If my name was Ezekiel, my little China Girl, I would push you back down like this. And I would roll over on top of you like this. And then I would run my hand up you like this and kiss you like—"

Just then, right next to their heads, a tiny child's voice asked, "Is she hurted?"

Both adult heads swiveled sideways, and they saw a small child, not much past two. A little girl in dirty, footed pajamas, with tear streaks visible through the mud smear on her face. She was standing there holding a dirty rag doll by one of its legs.

In the silence, the little girl offered, "Mommy's hurted."

Not moving from their embrace, in their shock, it was Mab who finally asked, "Katy?"

The small child raised her head way up on its tiny neck then down to touch her chin to her little chest, all quite soberly done.

They moved. Rising, they reached for clothing. "How did you remember that?" Tris asked of Mab.

"Ken and Tracy Harris?" She said it as in question.

"Yes."

She asked Katy, "Are you hungry?"

Again the nod. But little Katy watched Mab and Tris with wary eyes. So sad but careful. "You...stranger?"

Ah, the mother warning. Calmingly Mab told the child, "We are here to help your mother."

"There." Katy pointed toward the glimmer of the lake.

They'd been that close! Mab was dressed again and shivering—whether from being naked or finally finding the child she didn't know. Obviously Tracy needed them.

Mab gave Katy a cup of the broth, which the child drank with great thirst. Mab had to hold the cup and keep her from taking too much. The baby eyes looked up at Amabel. "More."

Tris was dressed, shaking out their blankets and folding them into the Jeep. He kept out an egg sandwich, for Mab to feed the little girl. She quickly shared the other cup of broth with Tris before he stored the food. They would eat later. Amabel finished dressing as Tris urged, "Come along, I believe we can get closer."

But Katy wouldn't get into the Jeep. "Mommy say 'no.'" And very seriously Katy shook her head side to side.

Mab told Tris quickly, "Go ahead. I'll bring her down."

"There's another flashlight." Tris sounded hurried. "Here. And your bag, I'll carry that in the Jeep."

"Give the bag to me and go on," Mab suggested. "The mother is hurt badly enough that Katy has wandered off. She may be unconscious. Go on. I have some mints in the bag, pitch it out. We'll come along. If it gets too dark, turn on the Jeep lights, we'll see them. Call in!"

He was reluctant to leave her. "We're bigger. We can just put her into the Jeep."

With impulsive empathy, Mab understood that Katy had been through enough for one day—she needed her life to be as normal as they could manage, and she'd been told not to ride with strangers. Amabel said to Tris, "It's not far. She made it up here, we can make it down. It might be better if you get things started, and...check for vital signs before we get there?" She gave Tris a speaking look. The woman might be dead.

"Understood." He bent his head to kiss her mouth lightly. Possessively. And she lay her head briefly on his shoulder to hug him. She looked at him with her heart in her eyes. He touched her cheek, then climbed into the Jeep. "Don't be long."

It was still light enough to see. Tris would have to take the circuitous route. The Jeep eased off over the rough terrain. Tris could search out the Harris camp more quickly in the Jeep than on foot.

But Amabel was suddenly lonely out there in the middle of nowhere. She picked up the flashlight and her bag. She hunted through the bag and found the small box of mints. They were soft, after-dinner mints. They were sugar. "Hold them in your mouth and let them melt."

"Candy?"

Don't take candy from strangers! "A mint. It's okay." She held out the mint on her hand.

Uncertain, Katy studied her. Amabel didn't say anything and just allowed the child to take her time. What would Tris find?

Mab's eyes turned to the swath cut across the trees by the fury of one of the tornadoes that had touched down. She looked at the twisted and torn limbs that exposed the white raw wood of the trees. And the power of the storm made her spine shiver. "Come, Katy. We'll go find your mother."

Katy stood still, deciding. Amabel walked slowly away down the hill and stopped before she looked back. Katy was a lonely, tiny being there on that empty hill. Amabel held out her hand.

Tris was some time getting to the lake. The natural water drainage gullies that scored the slope were a hindrance. He blundered onto the tree-studded slope that had sold the Harrises on the land, and went over the uneven ground to the lake.

There was no car. The parked trailer hadn't been lashed down, and it was strewn across some distance. Whole walls had been blown into trees, and some of it was in the water. If they had been inside...

He stopped the Jeep and called out. "Ken? Tracy? Can you hear me?"

There was no reply.

Calling frequently, he began to search. He saw car tracks. Had someone left? Taking the mother? Would they have left the child? Perhaps someone had come along and not known the child was in the woods? Or the little girl had hidden from strangers?

There were no bodies floating in the lake that he could see. He began a systematic search. Hearing footsteps in the brush he turned. "Harris?"

Two men emerged and, having heard Tris's calls, they were not surprised to see Tris. They had guns. Something about them made Tris cautious. "Have you seen anything of the people who were in this trailer? We're searching for them." He made his voice easy, calming and normal—as Sean Morant would with an unruly crowd ready to explode.

The heavier of the two gave him a neutral, dismissive look and said, "They left."

The other asked, "Yer Jeep?"

"No."

"Ya gah the kez?"

Tris didn't immediately reply. He began to worry about Amabel. She could walk in on this! The men were probably looters. Would they kill him? What would they do to Amabel? "The Jeep was loaned to me. I am one of those who is checking on people for injuries. Locating, helping."

"Gimme da kez t' da Jeep."

The Jeep was expendable. Tris had called in their location to the emergency station; if they didn't report back, someone would come to see why. He wanted those men gone from there before Mab came.

Still calm, Tris agreed, "If you need the Jeep, go ahead. When you're finished with it, arrange to deliver it to the courthouse in Columbia City." He was unthreatening, making everything appear normal. "Leave the first-aid kit and several of the blankets."

Without any other word, the two men got into the Jeep. As the driver started the motor, the other guy pitched the first-aid kit to Tris and flung out two blankets. Their progress was slowed by the mud, but the Jeep moved on through it and up the hill.

Tris stood and watched, then eased back to the shelter of the trees. He needed to find Amabel. What if the two men came back? What if they didn't want to leave someone who could give a description of them? What could he tell about them?

The two men were obviously looters, not scavengers and they weren't from around there. They had absolutely no fear in them, therefore they knew they wouldn't be recognized. They had on army surplus jackets, hunting caps, denims and boots. They looked just like most other men. Nothing unusual. They were semibearded since they hadn't shaved for a while.

What would they do with the Jeep?

Tris wasted no time stepping farther into the trees. He picked up a stout branch, arming himself... against guns? And finally he saw that the Jeep had made it quite easily through the mud, up over the hill and out of sight.

Tris could be shot from ambush from above. Where was Amabel, his Mab? Would she have heard any of it? What would she think, with the sound of the Jeep leaving? That he'd left her there alone? Surely she would know he wouldn't run off and leave her? She had a flashlight and some mints—and a small child to worry about.

He had to find them. Mab had to be warned. But first he had to know that Jeep was gone and the two men wouldn't come back. He looked at the wreckage of the trailer. A microwave. A generator. A television. A computer.

They could well come back.

He listened to the Jeep as he started through the trees in a gully at one side of the slope, and he moved toward the high ground to watch. Then the Jeep's motor stopped. There was a silence that chilled Tris. He gripped the club he'd found. He walked carefully, stalking. He wondered if he and Mab had any time at all left to them. Where was she? Had they found her? He moved forward, a hunter now.

Another motor started. And as he watched from the trees, a pickup came into sight. A four-wheel-drive, it moved easily over the crest, hesitated as the same two men looked around, then it eased down the slope to the wreckage.

One watched, with his gun ready, and the other chose from the selection of what was left of the Harris's possessions. He put it all into the bed of the pickup. Then, finished, they took the abandoned first-aid kit and flashlight, ignored the blankets and left.

Again Tris watched them. He heard the pickup pause. Then the Jeep's hood opened, as the two scavenged for parts. Finally he heard vehicle doors slam. And the pickup roared off, fading far into the silence of the distance, leaving the crippled, wheelless, gutted Jeep behind.

It was still light enough, and Tris went into the trees to hunt down Amabel. He found her footprints; she was carrying the child. He found where she hesitated, one smeared footprint with one footprint turned back. Had she heard the men? Or did she hear the Jeep leave? Then her prints moved away, down one of the thickly overgrown gullies. Carrying the child, her weight was enough to leave her prints. He risked a soft call, "Mab?" as he followed her trail.

About the third time, she replied, "Tris?"

Their meeting was emotional. She wanted to be against him, but she wouldn't let go of the child. He wanted her close enough—instantly—but then he had to look at her to reassure himself. But being against him was the shelter she wanted from him, and she resisted his separating from her, even slightly.

So he held her tightly. "My God." He said it as a prayer.

"I thought they were going to kill you for that Jeep."

"Me, too."

And she cried. Katy joined in easily, and Tris shook his head and laughed a ragged almost-laugh, which was filled with compassion.

"Who were they?" Mab asked.

"God knows. Looters. You were brilliant to hide. I'm so proud of you. Not a sound. You did exactly right."

"I wanted to shoot them." Mab was sober faced.

"You might have hit me." He smoothed her hair.

"I didn't have a gun," she explained.

"They did."

And she replied softly, "I saw."

Nine

Tris and Mab finally found Tracy Harris. She was cradled in a bush. Badly hurt. They eased their jackets under her so that nothing poked her, then they covered her as well as they could with the blankets. While Tris went through the wreckage for salvageable plastic, or woolen cloth, Mab stayed with the injured woman. She held Katy on her knees and talked to Tracy soothingly as she held the unconscious woman's hand.

Katy watched her mother, as children do. "Mommy sleep?" She pointed to her mother so Mab would know who she spoke about.

"She's hurt." It was better to say so.

"No open eyes." Katy's fat little fingers pushed up her own eyelids.

"We'll get help." How? The skeleton Jeep had no wheels and no longer held a CB. They were isolated out there. Had Tris called in before the Jeep was taken from him?

It was then she heard the chopper. She released Tracy's hand. Still holding Katy, she stood and ran clumsily toward the trailer remains. "Tris! Listen!"

He jerked around, startled in the new darkness. He held their remaining flashlight, beaming it upward toward the sky, waving it in a circle.

The chopper came closer, louder; Mab put Katy into his arms, then ran back to Tracy. She squatted, holding Tracy's hand in both of hers, and said, "It's a helicopter. We're trying to signal it. Katy's all right. I'm here. You'll be all right."

The sense of hearing is last to go and first to return, and Mab could imagine the confusion of a woman waking, after a tornado had thrown her into a bush and obviously concussed her. They hadn't dared to move her as yet to find what other injuries she might have. They only knew she was alive.

Anxiously, Mab looked skyward. In all that dark land, could the chopper see their tiny pinpoint of light? Was it looking for them? She strained, mentally guiding the chopper's observer to look their way.

Would the flashlight batteries last? And again she held Tracy's hand.

It was so dark. With the clearing sky, she could see stars. But the ground with its convolutions and trees must be a blank mass to the chopper. And it was cold. She shivered. Tracy's hand was cold. Was she dead? Mab listened fearfully and felt for a pulse in Tracy's wrist.

The chopper was closer. It would fly right over them. Would they look down? Mab wanted to stand up and wave her arms and yell. How could they see her? How could they possibly hear her over their own noise?

But the urge was so impulsively strong not to just sit there, but to signal. How? Build a fire? Why hadn't they thought to build a fire? That was the first thing stranded, shipwrecked people did. *A signal fire!*

She released Tracy's hand and felt for her bag. She'd left it somewhere around there. She searched, crawling, frantic. And found it. Blindly, her hand rooted inside for matches. She always carried matches. A leftover impulse from three years ago when she had quit smoking.

The flashlight was so feeble in that expanse of darkness. Her eyes were briefly glued to the running lights of the helicopter. Could she get a fire started in time?

Everything was still wet. She began to breathe harshly in her emotional, urgent hurry. She scrabbled around looking for anything burnable. She should move away from Tracy! The poor woman didn't need burns additionally...

The sound of the chopper was right overhead and it was loud! They *had* to look down. She had to get the fire going! She had to find something to burn! She was so intent on that, she didn't look up again.

She was shredding her checkbook and what cash she carried as the helicopter landed on the upper slope.

She looked at it quite stupidly; the blade was still whirling in the pool of its landing lights. It was there! It had seen that little flashlight? She squatted there over her little pile of tissues, shredded checkbook and money.

Somehow, in that strained time, the thought came. Wasn't there some law about not abusing money? She might go to prison. She would say, *"Well, I had to start a fire to signal the helicopter. Tracy Harris was—"*

And the government prosecutor would say snidely, *"But the paper isn't burned. You've made some critical remarks about your government. Are you sure you weren't tearing up that money to get some kind of perverted revenge?"*

Her mind went barreling along as her eyes witnessed men dropping from the landed chopper carrying things.

And up on the hill were cars. A police car and a wrecker and two other cars! Where had they all come from?

It was like Grand Central Station all of a sudden!

The figures moved down the hillside, and Mab went back to holding Tracy's hand. "They're here," she told the unconscious woman. "You're going to be put in a helicopter. You'll be all right."

The men had great, powerful lights, of which a single beam could light up the entire facade of a three-story house. They lighted that whole slope and, directed by Tris, the rescuers came trotting down the slope toward Mab. To Tracy.

Mab stood up and aside. Only one spoke to her. "You okay?" She nodded. After that, they extricated Tracy from that bush with exquisite care, supporting every joint, every vertebra. They put her on a stretcher. Tris's and Mab's jackets were returned to them, before the men carried Tracy up that slope more slowly, so they wouldn't joggle her. And they took Katy with them.

One of the Guards was a woman. The rescuers were from the National Guard. The tornadoes' damages had been so extensive that they had been called out to help.

It wasn't until the helicopter had taken off and faded into the sky, leaving them alone there on the ground, that Mab wondered, what about them? What would happen to them?

Tris took her in his arms and held her, kissing her in front of the cop, from special services and crowd control, who walked up with his light discreetly on the ground. Tris hugged Mab to him as the man said, "Heard you've been having an interesting time." He swept his impressive light over what was left of the trailer. "Too bad."

"Could they tell how badly Tracy Harris was hurt?" Mab asked.

"She's alive," Tris replied.

The cop nodded in agreement. "That's your Jeep," the cop confirmed something he knew. "You don't need a ride?"

"What are they doing?" Amabel finally looked up over to the activity that was going on under the lights of the wrecker.

"Tris, here, was clever enough to stick a twig into the CB to hold down the speaker."

"I did that when I was driving. I needed both hands to drive over that ground and I needed to get my call in about finding the Harrises."

The citizen cop nodded and picked up the story, "Emergency Headquarters listened to the whole thing. We roadblocked and caught the looters by surprise, and they gave up just like that. They are now replacing everything they took from the Jeep. They robbed two other places. After they return everything else, and apologize, then they'll go to jail."

Mab was surprised. "Apologize?"

"Our leader takes a dim view of crooks. They hurt and inconvenience people, and he makes them apologize."

"What a perfect beginning of their punishment. They scared us."

"Dumb. Both of them."

"I'm glad you caught them," Mab said. "They took the first-aid kit."

"It was Tris that made the catch easy. We need all the help we can get," the cop said grimly. "We're still ahead, and we'll stay that way, but it helps when civilians give us a signal to follow."

They watched the activity around the Jeep from a distance. The wrecker's lights made a stage setting in the night's darkness. The prisoners were in leg irons. They still moved well enough. The guards were patient and alert. And the wrecker driver was supervising the replacement quite meticulously. No tricks.

The cop mentioned, "They ate your supplies. But we've some extra. Are you hungry?" He led them to his squad car, dug out some food and left them there, as he went back to watch the prisoners.

Tris and Mab sat in the squad car to eat. Tris watched her, his eyes drawn to her, and she saw that was so. Obviously she watched him in order to see his constant regard of her. She smiled at him, and he leaned to kiss her.

"You never got scared," she said to him.

"I was scared."

"I was trying to light a fire."

"Excellent. Are you all right now? Someone ought to stay here to meet Ken Harris if he isn't contacted. You can imagine what it would be like for him to come here, see the demolished trailer and find his wife and baby missing. Being a stranger, he might not know who to contact right away, and it would be some time before he'd find out where they are. I've volunteered to stay so if he comes back, he'll know right away what happened. Will you stay with me?"

Her tender eyes rested on him and she smiled just so faintly, it was almost no smile at all. "I would love to stay here with you."

The looters had finished with the Jeep. The motor worked, the wheels were back in place and the rest of the contents were returned to it—the flashlight, the first-aid kit—everything except the food. Their blankets were added.

It made the looters mad to have to apologize. The older special services cop leaned his meager bottom on the Jeep fender and said, "We got all the time in the world. You did wrong, you apologize."

The scruffy looters looked at each other, then together they said, "We're sorry," with mean, insincere mouths.

Mab couldn't give the courteous reply and was silent. It was Tris who said, "We accept your apology."

One after the other, the vehicles left and finally Tris and Mab stood alone on the hill, watching the car and truck lights wind their way into the night.

It was so quiet.

"Can you shoot?" he asked her.

"Oh, yes. Rifles, shotguns, skeet shots, handguns. Father said everyone should know how. He's anti-Canadian and—"

"Nobody's *anti*-Canadian!" Tris was shocked.

"Father is. He is perfectly logical about everything else. Mother says we all need a flaw, and that's Father's. We don't know what started it, but not even the Russians made him as mad as the Canadians do now. He's sure they're going to invade."

"*Us?*" Tris began to laugh.

"I know. But he thinks they'll get cold, in the coming ice age, and they will begin to infiltrate and then the U.K.

will try to take us over. A resurgence of the empire syndrome."

Tris put his head back to laugh. And watching him, Mab smiled, too. "You should hear him when the Canadians complain—with all good reason—about acid rain. He is shocking."

"What sort of children do you suppose we'll have? The Magees are very typical of my side, and with you the daughter of a man who could be eccentric enough to be anti-*Canadian!*" He laughed again.

"Children?"

"Of course. I told you we would marry when I met you in the hall at the hotel in Indianapolis. Have you forgotten?"

"Not that. But you must admit we've known each other for a very short time, and you still don't know anything about my father's brother."

"Don't worry, I can probably match your weird—uh, eccentric relatives. I have a few, too."

She soothed him. "Somehow it doesn't surprise me that you have eccentric relatives."

"Now, why would you say that? Why would you think I'm strange enough that you're not surprised I have some relatives who tend to be just a little different from the rigid norm?"

"You're impulsive, brave and a *Rock* star!"

"Now, Amabel," he cautioned her. "There's nothing wrong with Rock stars."

She began to laugh. She tried to smother her hilarity, as he sputtered, and he finally solved it by kissing her. It did shut her up. When he allowed her to breathe, she said, "Thank goodness we have the first-aid kit."

That made him hesitate before he asked, "The first-aid kit?"

"And the instruction book," she explained.

He laughed softly as he swatted her bottom. Then he rubbed her nice bottom. His hand slowed and he kissed her again. Then again—and again. The playfulness vanished. The kisses turned hungry and earnest. His arms tightened, holding her close, closer, closest.

They set the CB to the emergency station and put it where they could hear it. Then with hot glances and touches, they made their bed near the Jeep. On the ground, they put the plastic from one wall of the trailer, then the ground sheet and the blankets. In the cool wind, they undressed and crawled quickly into their nest.

They lay shivering in their heating embrace and kissed hungrily. He lifted his head to look at her face faintly revealed in the stars' light. His voice was huskier than usual as he told her, "You're the most precious woman in all this world."

"Oh, Tris." She moved one hand to his nape to pet him and gently fingered his face, touching him with something akin to awe. She said, "I can't believe you're here."

"Ummm." He nuzzled her throat and moved his hot hand on her cool, bare body.

"I was terrified," she confessed to him. "I saw them. And their guns. And I tried to think what to do."

His voice roughly gruff, he replied, "I prayed you would hear us, and at least hesitate long enough to know the danger to you."

Her hand moving gently on his face, she shook her head in her real amazement. "You were so calm."

"Not at all." He turned his head and kissed her caressing hand. "I was savage inside. It even made me aware how primitive I felt about you being in danger. I wanted those men gone." As he kissed her, he gathered her against him. His hands pushed under her so that his arms were wrapped around her supine body, holding her up to him. And his kiss was ferociously possessive.

He broke the kiss. His arms gently released her, in order to free his hands to explore her. His hands were as possessive as the kiss had been.

She watched his face as he leaned up to look down her body and she explained what had happened, there alone in the gully. She told him, "I had Katy. I didn't know what to do. If I had put her down and tried to help, she might have followed."

"When I saw your footprints," he said, his voice rasping, "I remembered reading about imprints preserved for hundreds and hundreds of years. It was the small, bare foot of a woman. Her prints walked along in the solidified, primal clay, and at one point she stopped, and her prints showed she had looked back along the way she'd come." His hand on the opposite side scooped her closer to him, but it was again possessive.

He went back to their exchange. "The archaeologists speculated why the woman had turned to look back." His mind was seeing Mab's flight very clearly. "All that long ago. Why had she turned to look back? To call to someone? No prints followed hers. Her pace didn't change, she wasn't fleeing. Was she just being cautious? Her prints were too deep, as would be indicated for body weight, for her stride and such a slender foot, so she had to be carrying something. A child?

"And I saw your prints in the mud." His hand moved to cup the back of her head. "And you, too, turned to look. I could see it in your footprints. And you carried a child. It amazed me how primitive I felt over your footprints. To follow you and find you. You're mine."

His kiss was filled with passion, but there was more. There was that new, intense possession, the need, the hunger, but something more. His lovemaking became a storm of desire. His body's heat was scorching to her warming flesh; his hands were hot, his breath was ragged and his mouth scalding as he moved his face down her thrilled, writhing body.

Her fingers were in his hair, and on his shoulders. Her body was twitching, as little squeaks sounded in her throat. Her body heated, and then flamed until her own sweat of passion filmed her eager flesh. The two slid together, their bodies hot and slick with their passionate need. Earnestly she gasped, "If you back out on me this time, Ezekiel, I'll throttle you!"

He replied, equally serious, "I'll marry you after our seventh child, my little China Girl."

"She must have loved him." She was straining to Tris.

"Yes."

"Tris, I love you."

"Me, too."

Their kiss then was entirely different again. It was a mating of their very souls. Lying out there under the night sky, their hands were gentle, their mouths sweetly loving, and their kiss was profound.

But then it deepened, and the passion became intense. Their bodies pressed and slid, and their hands moved. Their need raged in them, and they came together in an explosion of passion; there was a brief pause as her barrier was broken, then he hesitated in order to ease it for her. He shuddered with the emotion, and she wept a little. He comforted her with shaking hands and sweet kisses, then he began to move.

It was all so strange and different for her, that she was distracted from her desire. She was conscious of his marvelous body, the musculature, the feel of him. Her thighs were aware of the size of him, lying on her as she moved her legs along his hair-textured thighs. She felt his hairy torso on her. And her breasts knew his weight. Her hands moved on his head and back, and her tongue tasted his sweat.

It wasn't long before he gasped and groaned, his body rigid as he climaxed, and at last he collapsed onto his forearms, his sweaty face and scratchy beard buried in the haven by her neck and shoulder. "Oh, my Mab. I tried to wait for you."

"It's beautiful!"

"Ah, honey." He levered himself up so that he could prop his weight better, and relieve her of most of it, but he didn't separate from her. He kissed her face in tiny kisses, his breath still roughened. "I am sorry."

"Silly, it was beautiful. And so interesting. Books don't really tell you what it'll be like."

"Did I hurt you?"

"I'm amazed it actually fits."

"Now that *is* beautiful." He grinned. "You are amazing."

"How can I be amazing when I know you must not have been a virgin, too?"

"I never felt that...this. Mab, my love." His voice was huskier and low in his chest, making it vibrate into hers.

"How soon can we do it again?"

He laughed a little helplessly. "You're a madwoman. Wild and mind-bending. You seem so prim and proper and look at you! I heard you were a man hater! Aren't you being a little friendly for a man hater?" He pressed against her to indicate how friendly she was.

"Only men call me a man hater. I just never went the singles, bar-hunting circuit. I wasn't interested in relationships or one-night stands. So men decided I didn't like men.''

"And you like me?''

"Yes.'' She laughed and rumpled his sweaty hair.

He moved his whiskers under her jaw to kiss and lip-nip along there. She turned her head to give him more room. Her arms went up over his shoulders and her palms smoothed along the muscles of his back. He tongued her ear, and she moved her legs to clench his hair-roughened thighs. He lifted his mouth just enough for a whispered inquiry against her ear, with his breath disturbing the fine hairs that lay there. "Do you like that?''

"It's...very interesting,'' she gasped as her fingers dug into her hair at the back of his head.

She hadn't been satisfied. And he simply toyed with her. Since he was not so needful now, he took great pleasure in arousing her. And the extent of her passion stirred his. He turned them over, so he lay on his back, with her sprawled on top of him. She found that felt rather insecure, but gradually she became quite adventuresome.

She rubbed her chest on his then sat up as she took sassy control of their lovemaking, and she boldly took what kisses she wanted, while limiting his. She tapped his seeking hands with little slaps, but allowed her own their freedom. With the starlight, she could see the fires building in his eyes even as she felt his sex stir.

Knowing full well what she was inviting, she continued her torment. She ran her hands as she would, she nibbled and suckled his nipples, she tongued his ear, and put his hands by his head and admonished that he keep them there.

She swirled her hips, tightened muscles and laughed, as his breathing roughened. She sat perfectly still as he coaxed her. Then she would move just a very little bit to tease.

He lasted well, having been sated. But the time came that he simply took her hips, lifted her from him and lay her down. Then his torment began as he drove her right up a nonexistent wall.

When he finally took her again, it was fantastic. They rode to paradise, which was off the edge of all things real, into a realm of exquisite sensation. And they lay clutched together, shuddering under the impact of the afterthrills. That was marvelous, and they sighed as the turmoil faded into echos of completion.

Wrapped together in their primitive cocoon on the basic ground, they slept.

Tris was already up and into trousers and shoes when Mab heard a car. It was still dark. She sat up and was shocked to see a rifle in Tris's hand. Where had that come from? Then he gave her a handgun. "This is the safety. Stay down."

He pulled on his jacket and went to the Jeep to wait in the darker shadow of its protection.

The car stopped, the door opened and a man emerged. The new arrival was so intent, he didn't even see the Jeep. His headlights were pointed down the slope, where the ruins of the trailer were revealed.

Tris called, "Hello! I'm an emergency volunteer, who are you?"

The man turned, "I'm Ken Harris. *Where's my family?*" And the terror was in his voice.

"They're alive. We've waited for you. Take it easy." And Tris turned on the flashlight and put the gun into the Jeep.

Ken Harris had gone back to Detroit to tie up loose ends. He'd been driving since he heard how bad the tornadoes were, and he hadn't been able to get through on the phone.

While Mab dressed, the two men used the CB to call the emergency station in Columbia City, who called the hospital for a report.

Tracy was still alive at Lutheran Hospital in Fort Wayne. She had a concussion, but her vital signs were good. She was suffering from a broken arm, wrenched leg, three broken ribs, exposure and various abrasions and contusions. Ken was welcome to come to her whenever he arrived.

"What about the baby? What about Katy?"

The question was relayed, and the hospital replied. She, too, was there. She was asleep, and only under observation as a precaution. There was no evidence that she had sustained any harm, but they were taking care of her.

Tris and Mab shared their food with Ken, making him relax. Reassuring him. Telling him of all the people who had searched for the Harris family.

As they talked, Ken's appetite asserted itself. The pressure he'd been under all day had caused him such tension that his entire concentration had been to get there.

He related, "The damage along the way is unbelievable! There are trees that look like crews had stripped them ready for a lumber cutting. How could a tree be wrecked?

"I saw barns that were blown apart. Wood high in the branches of trees. And all the lines down. A whole house was scattered like matchsticks!" And he looked down the slope to what was left of the house trailer.

"And a great marching power line's carriers were twisted like tinker toys." Ken wondered how the telephone men would ever get it all sorted out. It had scared him. "All I could think of was Tracy and Katy. They are so little and delicate. I looked at all the destruction, and I was scared. I had to get here. I've got to see Tracy and Katy."

"Do you want us to go with you?"

"No, thanks, I'll be okay now. They're both alive, and adrenaline is pumping through me so I'll stay awake." But he couldn't quit talking. He couldn't quit after so long a time of being alone with all the worry and terror. He said, "I heard 'tornadoes,' up there in Detroit, but I don't know this area so well, yet, and I had trouble figuring it out. My God. Did you see our trailer?"

"It was looted, but the looters were caught and the stuff is at Columbia City and labeled with your name. You'll at least get that back."

"I can't thank you enough."

"A lot of people helped. We were only two of many."

Ken shook his head in the helpless way of helpless people. "I don't know how to thank them all."

Tris assured Ken, "You did when you called the emergency station just now. You did it well. They'll spread the word."

Ken was looking down the hill to the scraps, which were all that was left of their trailer home. "You get so wrapped up in your own life, you forget how good people are."

"Yes. We do, too."

Ken said, "Well, I'll go on. You were very kind to wait for me here. I don't know what I would have done without you here to meet me. That was especially kind."

"We didn't want you to just walk in on it and not know what happened."

"Thank you."

"You're welcome." The shook hands, and Ken left, driving away through the predawn.

Tris put his arm around Mab's shoulder. "We aren't needed here now."

But she asked, "Where did you get the guns?"

"Oddly enough," Tris told her, "they're the looters' guns. The special services cop seemed to think it would be smart to have something on our side."

"It was," Mab agreed. "I'm glad you stayed here to waylay Ken. You handled it just right."

"So have you. I'm to return the guns to the police station when we leave here."

"Uhhh." Mab leaned against Tris. "Do we have to go now?"

And Tris grinned, trying not to as he replied, "No."

"Good," Mab retorted quickly. Then she said, "Come to bed." It was a command.

He sighed elaborately. "I suppose you want another chance at my poor, helpless body?"

"I want some *sleep!* In these last several days, what with one thing or another, I haven't had any sleep at all."

He looked at his watch. "It's only 3:21, and you've been asleep for hours!"

"I'm going back to sleep." She marched over to the Jeep, peeled off her clothes and shivered into the blankets to huddle there. It was cold, and a little damp, but since the blankets were woolen, she would eventually warm up.

He came up and squatted by her. He put out his big,
rough hand to brush her hair from her face. He growled
in a low, husky voice. "Hey, woman, what are you doing in my bed?"

"I'm going to sleep!" She was firm in her announce-
ment. Then she shivered, pulling the blankets around her
head.

But she didn't sleep, not for some long time. He
stripped off his clothes and boots and picked up the side
of the blankets, letting in more cold March air, but then
he brought his heat to her. It wasn't long after he took
her back into his arms that the blankets were cozy and
warm again. Deliciously warm. Hot.

Had he been sleeping alone, he would have peeled
some of them back, but she was wrapped around him so
wickedly and so hot that he . . . just . . . gave up.

Ten

Their CB remained silent the rest of that night. The two strangers who had happened to be in the midst of a disaster weren't needed. The worst of the emergencies was past. Volunteers and the National Guard had worked long, hard hours to seek out and help anyone who needed it.

They would continue to help, demolishing houses and buildings that were no longer safe, clearing debris from the streets and helping people in the monumental task of cleaning up.

The ramifications of the storms would last for years—the injuries, those coping with the deaths and destruction. Lives were changed by that network of storms. And one of those lives was Amabel Clayton's.

In the first light of dawn, she wakened, lying against Tris's bare, cozy warm body. She smiled before she ever opened her eyes. As she yawned and stretched in minute movements, there was a rumble of humor inside the strong, furred chest under her ear.

Her lashes lifted and her blue blue eyes regarded him with sleepy candor. "Counting that afternoon in L.A., we've known each other for exactly four and a half days. We are shameless!" She actually blushed.

His hand moved from her shoulder to hug her head to him. Then his fingers idly pleasured themselves in her hair, feeling the silk of it, smoothing it from her forehead.

His deep, foggy voice was reasonable. "You have to remember I've been aware of you for three years. And you will agree it's been a very unusual four and a half days."

"Yes."

"In this short time, we've seen each other under stressful times, good times and peaceful times. We probably know each other better than people who've dated for a year."

He paused as he thoughtfully kissed her forehead. "Your concern for Katy touched me. You're brave. You're a great lady." He put his hand back to her shoulder and hugged her again, then the hand slid on down to feel the satin skin sheathing of her back.

"You want me to tell you how wonderful I think you are?" She swiveled her head up to look at him again.

He sighed at the burden of it. "I *suppose* I could handle a mention of it okay."

She told him, "You're awesome."

There was a slight pause, then he encouraged, "And...?"

"You'll allow me to say to you that you're a brave man, too?"

"If you insist."

She wiggled closer to Tris to tell him, "You're very brave."

"And...?"

Humor skipped in her words then. "Will you allow me a brief mention of what a fabulous lover you are?"

He sighed and covered a bored yawn. "I suppose, if you feel you must."

Laughter bubbling in her, she said, "Fantastic. I'm glad I didn't have you neutered."

That made him jerk and aloud, he demanded of her, *"What?"*

"When I saw the cover of *US* and finally realized it wasn't a staff, *Harvard Lampoon* type thing, I was going to have a veterinarian neuter you, being the dog you are. But I *am* glad I didn't."

He laughed. "I must agree! The picture of us is on my bedroom wall."

He kissed her quite thoroughly with rather rough male dominance, and she laughed. Then they sighed and lay quietly in their cozy nest.

She asked, "Did I ever get to tell you how much I love your song about Ezekiel and My Ling?"

He looked off as if he was suffering her neglect. "No, you never have."

"It was such a beautiful surprise. I was teary-eyed."

He gathered her back to him and said honestly, "I wrote it for you. Have you ever had a song written for you before?"

"No."

"Another first. Beside your first tornado, first Rock concert and the first lovemaking."

She elaborated the list. "My first seminar, first patrol in an emergency and first night sleeping out on the ground, sharing my bedding."

"And your first man. Your first serious love."

"Yes." The sound was almost shy.

He nudged her chin up and leaned his head down to his chest to give her a nice fat squishy smacking kiss that was quite smug.

She was so contented, lying there snuggled in his arms, her naked body curled around his, warm and toasty from the heat of him. She moved her hand through the hair on his chest, enjoying the feel of his strong, vibrant body.

After their silence, in the peace of the very early morning, he asked, "Beside me, what's shocked you the most?"

With her fingers, she tugged on his chest hair, and he laughed. He clarified his question. "I just meant what's been the most unusual of these unusual days—besides me."

He gestured minutely, "I don't want to have to listen to you carry on and on and *on* about what a fabulous lover I am, and how I sent you to the skies and all that sort of thing. I'm more curious about your journalistic comparison and contrasts of tornadoes and Rock concerts."

She readily replied, "Actually there are similarities."

He scoffed. "I was being funny."

"As an impartial witness," she lectured. "There are similarities."

He snorted in rejection.

She hushed him as she continued, "Both are shocking, noisy and soon over, leaving the witnesses exhausted and a litter of debris on the site. All very disruptive.''

He instructed, ''Rock concerts are exciting, while tornadoes are terrifying.''

''In another way, so is that mass of arm-waving teenagers. They look like a field of waving arms.''

''Our crop of the future.''

''True,'' she agreed. ''And hearteningly, a good crop. As I've been going around the West Coast for *Adam's Roots*, I've found the great majority of kids are really terrific. And yesterday, I saw how people are impulsively kind and helpful to others. It was almost overwhelming. And then in sharp contrast, there were those two men.'' She shuddered.

He moved his other arm and shifted his body to hold her more securely. ''Every once in a while, it's brought to our attention how chancy life can be. A near miss on a highway, a sudden serious illness, seeing a place destroyed by a tornado, or two men who aren't civilized enough to care about anyone else.''

Musingly, he continued. ''But such things do make you value life more. And it will make you more conscious of your need for other people. We all share this planet.''

She became really serious and one hand slid along his face in such a sweet caress. ''I really love you, Tris.''

''I'm glad,'' he replied gently. ''I love you. I want to live with you and be your love and make babies with you. Will you marry me?''

She frowned and shared her feelings. ''It troubles me that I am so strongly for women's rights, and yet I find myself out here in this primitive location, naked, in your arms. And—right now—I am perfectly willing to forget my job and all it means to me, and say yes to whatever you want.''

He shifted even more until he was on one elbow above her. She thought how typical: He's in the dominant position, and I'm in the submissive one.

Tris's free hand brushed her hair back and his eyes were serious. "And I'm ready to adjust my life to however we can manage so we can be together. We just have to figure out the details. We both need some things—I want music, and you love your job. If we do this right, we can find a way for us both and share our lives.''

She was so touched by him, she leaked tears. He was in earnest. After all that talk about male superiority! And here he was, ready to bend, too! But could they?

They had seen each other under such strange and tumultuous circumstances, and they had both measured up without a blink of hesitation. But what about the ordinary, grinding, day-to-day living? Could their regard for each other survive the basic life of the nitty-gritty?

It was easy for people to be carried away on the high of the emotion caused by crisis. Just the impulse to survive could trigger the clutch at security. And being glad to survive, all sorts of noble intentions could seem to be solid.

What if ordinary life ground down on them and drove them wild with boredom and frustration? The only way to prove that was by the old, tried way of spending the time to really know each other, instead of impulsively committing their lives on the peak of the wave of excitement and passion.

Her tears spilled over. She told him, "I never cry."

His smile melted her more. "I know. You are so female, you are fascinating.''

"I have no idea why I cry around you, but that's about all I seem to've done since I met you—for one reason or another." And she suddenly wondered. Was it a secret knowledge that they were actually unsuited? That this could very well turn out to be only an interlude?

Tris told her, "You've had me a little inside out, too, you know. I want to put stars in your eyes and make you love me."

"I do love you." In spite of her confusion, was she trying to convince him of her love even if they would be parted?

He leaned slowly to kiss her, and her welcome was so poignantly sweet. Their lovemaking, then, was of another, more gentle, cherishing kind, and their need wasn't as explosive. He worshiped her body and she became more knowledgeable about his. Their touches were more refined and deliberately titillating, but their completion was no less thrillingly satisfying.

Again they slept, and their naked bodies were entwined. As she drifted into sleep, Mab wondered if the time would come when she'd sleep alone. It would probably happen. Sober faced, she listened to his deep, steady breathing. Her breaths paced his. And she, too, slept.

The CB wakened them some time later; Tris rose from their blankets and went to the Jeep to reply. The emergency base was just checking up on all its volunteers to see if everything was all right.

The base reported, "Your Aunt Trudy says Ken Harris and his daughter Katy are coming to their house. That way there'll be someone around to take care of the baby until Mrs. Harris is out of the hospital. She's doing okay.

"And your Rock group has been around helping. They're a nice bunch. They got panicky about you and gathered around. They're headquartered with your aunt, too."

"They're all there?"

"Yeah. Nice bunch." He seemed a little surprised since he repeated it.

"Thanks. Whistle if you need us."

"Right. Base clear."

Tris put the CB back in the Jeep and standing there he turned toward Amabel. He was gloriously naked. His body's symmetry was beautiful, and his musculature was marvelous to see. He was total maleness. He smiled at her regard, and then he stretched, quiet leisurely, deliberately showing off.

It was a pleasure to see him. He was almost like a rooster crowing to start the day. He was magnificent. His movements were slow and sensually relished. Then he stood with his hands on his bare hips, and he surveyed the entire area. Arrogantly male.

And she curled, protected, in blankets still warm from the heat of his body, and she was softly female and watching him.

Having looked over the land, he turned back to her and his eyes were possessive and contented. She had to smile a little. He was actually a very basic man. He grinned at her. "Come, woman, let's take our morning's plunge in the lake."

She replied tartly, "You're totally mad."

"It'll be invigorating!"

"It would be *pneumonia!* I'll wait right here. You go ahead."

With his hands on his hips and his feet apart, his head came a little forward as he commanded, "Come along, now. Shake a leg. Hit the deck. Rise and shine."

She laughed out loud, very amused. She knew exactly what his ancestors had been like all those thousands of years ago, and she was glad they had survived. She clutched the blankets to her one last time, then threw them back to burst from the bed and run down the slope to the lake.

He whooped, exhilarated, and ran just a little behind her so that he could watch her naked body in its madly exuberant flight. He laughed, so free, but she shrieked over the mud at the edge of the lake and faltered. He simply scooped her up and carried her on into the lake and threw her farther.

It was like liquid *ice!* She barely rinsed off, it was so cold! But he splashed and coaxed and ran her around, chasing her with wicked touches, quick squeezes and pats while she shrieked in squeaks and laughter, until she warmed enough to play. With vigorous swimming, they could stay in for a while, and they began to envy the Harris family for their Eden. Their newly tangled Eden.

At last, holding hands, the lovers trudged up the slope and used one blanket to towel off. They dressed their glowing bodies. They hungrily finished the sandwiches and apples the cop had shared with them the night before. The coffee by then was terrible.

With some reluctance, they slowly drove back into town, back to reality. They filled the Jeep tank with gas and returned it to the emergency station. An idle volunteer drove them back to the Magees' house, and stayed, because there were so many people there.

Aunt Trudy was in her element, feeding, nurturing, scolding and taking care of people. It *is* an ill wind that bodes no good. And some gleaners who reaped good from those devastating tornadoes, were the musicians and a few of the Roadies who'd come so briefly to Fort Wayne with Tris. For them, it was an adventure. They'd been out and around, helping, hauling, delivering and eating.

When the Magees complimented them for their impulsive help, they replied, "It's real. We have to touch base with life occasionally or we think the Rock world is all there is."

The Hoosiers had welcomed the strangers among them, and the need for their help. The musicians had pitched in willingly, worked hard and gathered the reward of acceptance. Of involvement. And hardly anyone of those they helped had ever heard of their group!

One asked, "You make records?"

"Yep" was the amused reply of one Roadie.

The questioner commented, "That right? Country-western?"

They didn't dare to look at each other as their speaker gently replied that one disturbing word, "Rock."

With lips that parted soundlessly in shock, the listeners asked, "Like on MTV?"

"Yeah."

Then they'd be examined through narrowed, considering eyes. And there were those who adjusted their glasses for a clearer look at the guests. "You don't look that weird."

That's when the laughter came.

When the whole group decided they'd buy land and settle there, Finnegan Magee cautioned, "Do you remember *The Music Man?* And the song about the Iowans standing toe to toe for a week and never seeing eye to eye? Iowa was settled by people who moved west from Indiana when Indiana first got too crowded a hundred years ago.

"We rally around for a crisis, and after the trouble has passed, then the closeness slides off into a casual wave. In a month, the area will be about its own business again, and the neighborliness will all calm down to casual, stiff courtesy."

The drummer said, "Yeah. But it's nice to know people pitch in when that crisis comes along."

And Finnegan's eyes twinkled. "Just like the bunch of you. You must be part Hoosier?"

They all laughed at the indignant way the Roadies declared their own home places.

They had a farewell party but it lasted so late they all stayed another day. Tris was assigned to sleep in the dormer with the other single men, and his Mab slept on a second-floor sleeping porch for single women.

Just feeding the mob of people was impressive, and it took a lot of work. Everybody pitched in and helped with it all. The visitors were like locusts devouring a field of corn. Tris saw to it the supplies were replaced.

The tree leaning against the side of Magees' house was finally cut down with chain saws and cut into firewood lengths and split. The musicians risked their talented hands at splitting the wood. That became competitive.

The visitors all called Tris' family Aunt Trudy and Uncle Finnegan, and relatives gathered around to share the fun. Everyone was "cousin," and they tried to coax the younger women into being "kissing cousins."

It was then it became area knowledge that Sean Morant was Tris Roald and the Magees related to Sean Morant. It meant absolutely nothing to a great number of people, but to those who knew who Sean Morant really was, it was a revelation and it made them smug to know a secret.

Through it all, Mab watched Tris and wondered how their lives would go.

Reality finally intruded. Tris had a recording deadline, and Mab had to go back to L.A. Their separation was emotional. She wondered how many more times, in the days to come, would she be held in his arms?

As she flew back to Los Angeles, alone, her mind chewed on her problems. Why was she so despondent? It was obvious she didn't think their love could survive.

He called her and each time he asked, "Are you okay?"

And she finally said, "Yes."

The spring passed and summer faded into fall as the lovers struggled to be together. There were the daily telephone calls at first, but there came the skipped day. Then it would be several days.

They complained about their schedules. The blip in contacting each other was always due to their work. They were both busy and their schedules were tight.

But they met in St. Louis, and spent the weekend in bed. He'd brought fruit, cheeses, bagels, cream cheese . . . and condoms. They laughed and loved, and it was another unusual time. No real test, just hungry eyes, and hands and bodies . . . sated.

They met in Denver, in Atlanta, in Chicago. She went to two of his concerts and watched the hype. How could he ever give up that adoration? How could she replace that worship? Could only one woman suffice? How?

Then there was the weekend planned and anticipated that didn't happen. And his surprise visit to L.A. to be with her... but she was in Seattle.

He groused over the phone, "I sat on your stoop for two hours before your sexy neighbor came over and told me you were gone."

"Did she console you?" Amabel snapped in question.

"Is that all you can say?"

She snarled at him, "What more do you want from me?"

"You could say you were lonesome up there in Seattle, and you wish you had been home."

After a silent minute, she told him, "I wish I had been there to open the door and put my arms around you."

"That's better."

Her voice uneven, she told him, "This isn't working out very well."

"There has to be a solution." But his voice was tired and he sounded distracted.

She said it again, "I can't give up my job."

His reply was repeated, "Nor I."

She started to cry again. He talked sweet things to her and groaned with his frustration. She went on crying.

It was all depressing. How could such attraction be so good and so impossible? She had been right not to rush into that impulsive marriage with Tris.

There were good reasons for rules of conduct. Control, propriety and abstinence were good rules.

She hadn't been able to wait to make love with Tris. How amazing he hadn't gotten her pregnant! He? She was a victim? What had she been doing out there in his blankets? She was responsible for herself and her own conduct. She couldn't blame anyone else.

She remembered him as he got up to answer the CB that early morning on the Harris's hill. How he'd stretched his magnificently naked body, knowing she watched him. And he'd allowed her to fill her eyes with the sight of him.

At the time, she'd been so amused by his strutting for her that she'd likened him to a rooster. But a rooster depended on feathers for his glory. Tris had only his own body. So beautiful. He was so marvelously male. His stretching had been so male animal, but a human male animal.

And she remembered herself lying warm and protected in those blankets still heated from his body.

She wanted to be with him. Soberly she finally faced the adjustments her life would have to take, in order to be with him. She was at a crossroads of choice.

It was then she really began to appreciate women. Really to appreciate them. Not the singular she, but all women. And pioneer women especially. The women all through the ages.

How many of them had wanted to leave their families and go out across the unknown? In all of time, how many of the women had been as curious as the men to see what was on beyond?

There were a good many pioneer women, in her own background, who had gone along, pitched in and made it all work. Was this day so different? No wagon train, but airplanes. No sod house but condos. Was it so different?

Amabel Clayton faced the fact that whatever it took, she was going to go to Tris and make it work. She went to her boss, Wally, and she explained her situation. She was going to resign her job.

He was amazed. "You love him that much?"

"Apparently." She wasn't very enthused. She'd run her own life for some time. She liked it, she answered to no one. Her life was her own way, as *she* wanted it.

What was in her closet was hers. What was in her refrigerator was what she wanted there. Her meals were when she chose and where she chose.

"You can free-lance," Wally suggested.

"Thank you."

"Your coverage last year of the tornadoes in Indiana was superb."

"It was a remarkable experience."

Wally looked on her as if she was having her period and was affected by the hormone imbalance. He advised, "Take a leave. Don't resign yet."

"Don't tempt me. I need to cut ties and really give this a chance."

"I'm impressed with you, Mab. I wonder if Chris would do this kind of thing for me."

Mab looked at him in surprise. "She did."

Wally frowned. "What do you mean?"

"She never told you about Paris?" Mab gestured in a chop.

He questioned softly, "Paris?"

Mab explained, "You two had had about three dates, and her boss offered her the Paris office."

"Oh, yeah!" His eyes snapped back to Mab. "She... turned it down... because of *me?*"

Mab nodded. "Without a flick of an eyelash. She said, 'If there's a chance with Wally, it's worth it.' At the time I thought her completely crazy." Mab paused. "She never told you?"

He searched him mind. "If she did, I didn't register it."

"She'd worked herself to her knees for the Paris office."

"My God," he said, and his eyes filled! "Can I use your phone?" Without waiting for her reply, he went right ahead. He punched in the number and waited restlessly as Amabel, too, could hear the ring and finally Chris saying, "Hello?"

"Honey, I love you."

There was a gasp and a snapped question.

"I'm fine. Get a sitter and let's go out to dinner tonight."

Mab could hear the sound of Chris talking.

Wally broke in on whatever Chris was saying, "I don't want to go. I'll call Bob and tell him something's come up. You and I are going to dinner. Wear that green thing. Chris, have I ever told you—I'll tell you tonight." He set the phone in its cradle and patted it twice. Then abruptly he said, "Thanks, Mab. And good luck."

Through tear-filled eyes, she watched him leave the room. She'd never cried before she knew Tris. Good heavens, what was happening to her? She was turning into a sentimental pushover.

She went home to pack. She looked around the apartment and acknowledged she probably would have to sell her carefully collected furniture. It would cost too much to send it all across the country. And she was a little surprised that she could do that—mentally relinquish her furniture with very little regret.

She understood finally that there was nothing she could have that matched her need for Tris. She had balanced everything in her life to the need for him, she had come to the conclusion when she relinquished her job. But it was the discarding of her furniture that finally made her realize he was the single most important thing in her whole world.

She was going to him. Free and clear.

The doorbell rang, and Mab went to it. She opened the peephole and stared at...Tris! She was stunned. She tore open the door and just stood there.

He was quite tired and a little grouchy. He was unshaven and rumpled. He said, "You win." He said that knowing full well that she'd never given him any kind of ultimatum.

He was startled to hear her burst into laughing tears! She flung herself at him. She rather annoyed him because, beside being exhausted and irritable, he was carrying wine and cheese, bagels and cream cheese, and a bag of oranges and apples.

Still weeping and gulping and blowing her nose, she helped him free of his packages and his heavy winter coat and still she wept...laughing.

"Are you hysterical?"

She shook her head.

In what sounded very close to being disgruntled, he grumped, "I can't live without you."

That only set her teary laughter off again.

Annoyed by then, he said, "You *could* handle it more graciously, you damn holdout."

She hugged him tightly, and he endured it with a resigned sigh. She leaned her head back and looked at his watery image and smiled so sweetly as she touched his face that he kissed her quite violently, his whiskered face rough on her tender skin.

His hard body held her soft one. His strong arms banded her like steel just like in a romance. And she gloried in it all. He was there!

He growled in her ear, "The damn plane was stuck in Kansas with ice for two days."

"Would you like a shower?" Her smile was almost idiotish, and her words wavered with her emotion and the stupid tears kept spilling over.

"Only if you take it with me. I've quit the group. We've been winding up. I was going to anyway." He did it for her. There was nothing in his life more important than she was to him. He needed stroking before he would admit it.

She helped him out of his clothes and he allowed her to valet him. She led him to the bath, holding his arm, and turned on the shower. He watched as she began to take off her own clothes and she smiled her silly, tremulous smile, blinking, trying to see him clearly.

He ducked under the spray, careless of how much water bounced off his head and shoulders and out onto the bath rug. He held her hand and helped her into the shower, then he stood as she washed him.

He began to relax, or maybe he wasn't all that relaxed, being as stiff as a board, but he began to be very very interested in being friendly with her. He began to wash her with gentle, caressing hands.

She exactly knew his problem. Besides wanting her, he loved her more than anything else in the world. She was so thrilled with that knowledge, and she could hardly wait until they went into the bedroom and he would see her bed.

They rinsed off and kissed in such a lovely way. She tugged his hand to leave the shower, but being the male animal he was, he lifted her to him, and took her there against the wall in the shower. She laughed. He needed her so badly that he was quickly completed. He leaned against the shower wall, his arms loosening finally to allow her to slowly slide from him.

It was then that he smiled at her. "It's been a bear cat of a trip. Everything that could happen wrong, happened wrong. I've been straining to get to you, Amabel, my Mab. I love you. It took forever. I've been mean to everyone in my way. Then I get here, and what did you do? You laughed in triumph."

She carefully dried his beautiful body, and he allowed her to do that as he went on talking. "I concede you've won. See if you can't be a good winner and not rub it in. I freely admit I'll do whatever you want of me, if you'll just marry me. But I think Ezekiel had the right idea. I should have just abducted you, China Girl, run off with you and kept you pregnant and locked up."

"Come into the bedroom."

"I'll go to sleep," he warned. "I'm exhausted. You're a damn hard women." By then they were back in the bedroom, and he saw the bed.

She looked up at him and her smile was melting.

He frowned furiously. "Where in the *hell* are you off to this time?"

"I quit my job, and I was packing to come to you."

The shock slowly registered as he understood. Then his eyes filled and he smiled. He took her into his arms and just held her. "We made it."

"Whatever comes..."

He wasn't exhausted after all, but held her for a long time, naked against his nakedness, cherishing her, before he removed all that impediment from the bed, rather haphazardly, and followed her into the enveloping covers.

They both knew that they really would make it, together, whatever did come.

*　　*　　*　　*　　*

SILHOUETTE® Desire®

COMING NEXT MONTH

MILLION DOLLAR SWEEPSTAKES (III)

No purchase necessary. To enter, follow the directions published. Method of entry may vary. For eligibility, entries must be received no later than March 31, 1996. No liability is assumed for printing errors, lost, late or misdirected entries. Odds of winning are determined by the number of eligible entries distributed and received. Prizewinners will be determined no later than June 30, 1996.

Sweepstakes open to residents of the U.S. (except Puerto Rico), Canada, Europe and Taiwan who are 18 years of age or older. All applicable laws and regulations apply. Sweepstakes offer void wherever prohibited by law. Values of all prizes are in U.S. currency. This sweepstakes is presented by Torstar Corp., its subsidiaries and affiliates, in conjunction with book, merchandise and/or product offerings. For a copy of the Official Rules send a self-addressed, stamped envelope (WA residents need not affix return postage) to: MILLION DOLLAR SWEEPSTAKES (III) Rules, P.O. Box 4573, Blair, NE 68009, USA.

EXTRA BONUS PRIZE DRAWING

No purchase necessary. The Extra Bonus Prize will be awarded in a random drawing to be conducted no later than 5/30/96 from among all entries received. To qualify, entries must be received by 3/31/96 and comply with published directions. Drawing open to residents of the U.S. (except Puerto Rico), Canada, Europe and Taiwan who are 18 years of age or older. All applicable laws and regulations apply; offer void wherever prohibited by law. Odds of winning are dependent upon number of eligible entries received. Prize is valued in U.S. currency. The offer is presented by Torstar Corp., its subsidiaries and affiliates in conjunction with book, merchandise and/or product offering. For a copy of the Official Rules governing this sweepstakes, send a self-addressed, stamped envelope (WA residents need not affix return postage) to: Extra Bonus Prize Drawing Rules, P.O. Box 4590, Blair, NE 68009, USA.

SWP-S1195

Who needs mistletoe when Santa's Little Helpers are around?

Santa's Little Helpers

brought to you by:

Janet Dailey
Jennifer Greene
Patricia Gardner Evans

This holiday collection has three contemporary stories celebrating the joy of love during Christmas. Featuring a BRAND-NEW story from *New York Times* bestselling author Janet Dailey, this special anthology makes the perfect holiday gift for you or a loved one!

FREE GIFT
with purchase
see inside

You can receive a beautiful 18" goldtone rope necklace—absolutely FREE—with the purchase of *Santa's Little Helpers*. See inside the book for details.

Santa's Little Helpers—a holiday gift you will want to open again and again!

Also available by popular author

LASS SMALL

Silhouette Desire®

#05800	BALANCED	$2.99	☐
#05817	*TWEED	$2.99	☐
#05830	A NEW YEAR	$2.99	☐
#05848	I'M GONNA GET YOU	$2.99	☐
#05860	SALTY AND FELICIA	$2.99 U.S.	☐
		$3.50 CAN.	☐
#05895	AN OBSOLETE MAN	$2.99 U.S.	☐
		$3.50 CAN.	☐
#05926	IMPULSE	$3.25 U.S.	☐
		$3.75 CAN.	☐

*Man of the Month

(limited quantities available on certain titles)

TOTAL AMOUNT	$
POSTAGE & HANDLING	$
($1.00 for one book, 50¢ for each additional)	
APPLICABLE TAXES	$_____
TOTAL PAYABLE	$_____
(check or money order—please do not send cash)	

To order, complete this form and send it, along with a check or money order for the total above, payable to Silhouette Books, to: **In the U.S.:** 3010 Walden Avenue, P.O. Box 9077, Buffalo, NY 14269-9077; **In Canada:** P.O. Box 636, Fort Erie, Ontario, L2A 5X3.

Name: _____

Address: _____ City: _____

State/Prov.: _____ Zip/Postal Code: _____

**New York residents remit applicable sales taxes.
Canadian residents remit applicable GST and provincial taxes.   SLSBACK6

Silhouette®
TM

CHRISTMAS WEDDING
by Pamela Macaluso

You're About to Become a

Privileged Woman

Reap the rewards of fabulous free gifts and benefits with proofs-of-purchase from Silhouette and Harlequin books

Pages & Privileges™

It's our way of thanking you for buying our books at your favorite retail stores.

```
┌ ─ ─ ─ ─ ─ ─ ─ ─ ─ ─ ─ ─ ┐
│      PROOF OF         │
        PURCHASE
│   Offer expires October 31, 1996  │
└ ─ ─ ─ ─ ─ ─ ─ ─ ─ ─ ─ ─ ┘
```
SD-PP75

Harlequin and Silhouette—
the most privileged readers in the world!

For more information about Harlequin and Silhouette's PAGES & PRIVILEGES program call the Pages & Privileges Benefits Desk: 1-503-794-2499

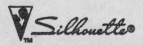

SD-PP75